FORGOTTEN
IN
DEATH

Titles by J. D. Robb

Naked in Death

Glory in Death

Immortal in Death

Rapture in Death

Ceremony in Death

Vengeance in Death

Holiday in Death

Conspiracy in Death

Loyalty in Death

Witness in Death

Judgment in Death

Betrayal in Death

Seduction in Death

Reunion in Death

Purity in Death

Portrait in Death

Imitation in Death

Divided in Death

Visions in Death

Survivor in Death

Origin in Death

Memory in Death

Born in Death

Innocent in Death

Creation in Death

Strangers in Death

Salvation in Death

Promises in Death

Kindred in Death

Fantasy in Death

Indulgence in Death

Treachery in Death

New York to Dallas

Celebrity in Death

Delusion in Death

Calculated in Death

Thankless in Death

Concealed in Death

Festive in Death

Obsession in Death

Devoted in Death

Brotherhood in Death

Apprentice in Death

Echoes in Death

Secrets in Death

Dark in Death

Leverage in Death

Connections in Death

Vendetta in Death

Golden in Death

Shadows in Death

Faithless in Death

Forgotten in Death

Anthologies

Silent Night
(with Susan Plunkett, Dee Holmes, and Claire Cross)

Out of This World
(with Laurell K. Hamilton, Susan Krinard, and Maggie Shayne)

Remember When
(with Nora Roberts)

Bump in the Night
(with Mary Blayney, Ruth Ryan Langan, and Mary Kay McComas)

Dead of Night
(with Mary Blayney, Ruth Ryan Langan, and Mary Kay McComas)

Three in Death

Suite 606
(with Mary Blayney, Ruth Ryan Langan, and Mary Kay McComas)

In Death

The Lost
(with Patricia Gaffney, Ruth Ryan Langan, and Mary Kay McComas)

The Other Side
(with Mary Blayney, Patricia Gaffney, Ruth Ryan Langan, and Mary Kay McComas)

Time of Death

The Unquiet
(with Mary Blayney, Patricia Gaffney, Ruth Ryan Langan, and Mary Kay McComas)

Mirror, Mirror
(with Mary Blayney, Elaine Fox, Mary Kay McComas, and R. C. Ryan)

Down the Rabbit Hole
(with Mary Blayney, Elaine Fox, Mary Kay McComas, and R. C. Ryan)

FORGOTTEN IN DEATH

J. D. Robb

ST. MARTIN'S PRESS
NEW YORK

FORGOTTEN IN DEATH. Copyright © 2021 by Nora Roberts. All rights reserved. Printed in the United States of America. For information, address St. Martin's Publishing Group, 120 Broadway, New York, NY 10271.

www.stmartins.com

Library of Congress Cataloging-in-Publication Data

Names: Robb, J. D., 1950- author.
Title: Forgotten in death / J.D. Robb.
Description: First edition. | New York: St. Martin's Press, 2021.
Identifiers: LCCN 2021016217 | ISBN 9781250272812 (hardcover) |
    ISBN 9781250272829 (ebook)
Subjects: GSAFD: Mystery fiction. | Suspense fiction.
Classification: LCC PS3568.O243 F674 2021 | DDC 813/.54—dc23
LC record available at https://lccn.loc.gov/2021016217

Our books may be purchased in bulk for promotional, educational, or business use. Please contact your local bookseller or the Macmillan Corporate and Premium Sales Department at 1–800-221-7945, extension 5442, or by email at MacmillanSpecialMarkets@macmillan.com.

First Edition: 2021

10 9 8 7 6 5 4 3 2 1

She lived unknown, and few could know
When Lucy ceased to be;
But she is in her grave, and, oh,
The difference to me!
—William Wordsworth

I do perceive here a divided duty.
—William Shakespeare

FORGOTTEN IN DEATH

1

For a homicide cop, murder often started the day. For the mixed-race female sloppily wrapped in a tarp and stuffed in a construction site dumpster, it had surely ended hers.

Lieutenant Eve Dallas ducked under the crime scene tape and strode across the demolition rubble. She'd already been on her way downtown to Cop Central when the call came through, detouring her to one of the construction sites in Hudson Yards.

The day had a soft feel to it, a breezy warmth as May of 2061 made way for June and the heat that would surely follow. Construction types stood around in their hard hats and steel-toed boots, gulping coffee, shooting the shit, and goggling at the dumpster where a couple of uniforms stood by.

Civilians, Eve knew, couldn't resist goggling at the dead.

She could hear the hard, staccato, machine-gun echo of an airjack at another site. The whole sector, she knew, was full of them.

The dumpster sat on the north side of the seventy-story spear of a building, on the edge where a trio of lesser towers huddled. The trio, post–Urban Wars toss-them-up-and-cross-your-fingers construction, showcased the dinge and wear of the years, the shrugged shoulders of neglect.

She noted broken windows, the pitted, graffiti-laced walls, crumbling facades, old beams now bent and twisted, and the big, muscular machines, the strangely delicate sway of the towering cranes, and the mountain range of lesser tools lined up to deal with them.

To her eye, it resembled the aftermath of a war zone, but the only casualty she could see lay wrapped in a dumpster like so much debris.

Whatever the plans, the schedule, the budget might be, it all stopped now.

The civilians could goggle at the dead, but she stood for them.

She carried her field kit to the cops at the dumpster, tapped her badge. "Who's first on scene?"

"That would be us, Lieutenant. Officers Urly and Getz."

"Run it for me," she said as she took a can of Seal-It from her kit.

Urly, a tall Black woman in her early forties, took the lead.

"Getz and I responded to the call at oh-seven-thirty-five. We confirmed the DB in the dumpster here, and secured the scene. The nine-one-one caller, a Manuel Best, stated he found the body shortly after he reported to work at seven-thirty."

"Maybe the blood trail gave him a clue."

Urly's lips twitched—the closest she got to a smile. "Yes, sir. Best stated he thought someone had dumped a dead or wounded animal in there."

"He's pretty shaken up, Lieutenant." Getz, white, husky, thirties, chin-pointed to the left. "Just a kid, college boy, summer job. Just started this week."

"Hell of a way to enter the workforce. I'll want to speak with him when I'm done with the body."

She stepped up, avoiding the drops of dried blood, and, a tall woman herself, peered into the dumpster.

She could see the side of the victim's head through the plastic sheeting. Scraggly hair, the color of dust, spilled over it. Blood matted the hair, smeared the sheeting.

Her hand fell out when the killer tossed her in, Eve thought. Rush job, bash, dump, run.

"Severe blunt force trauma to the right side of the victim's head is visible, as is a blood trail starting approximately four feet from the dumpster on the far side of the security fencing. Blood on the front of the dumpster, on the plastic sheeting used to cover the victim. Likely used to carry the victim to the dump site."

When she had the interior of the dumpster, the position of the body fully on record, she hissed out a breath.

She sealed up, passed her field kit to Getz.

And boosted herself into the dumpster.

Construction crap—not garbage, so lucky day. But construction crap could include nails, glass, toothy metal, and all kinds of sharps.

"She can't be more than five-two," Eve judged as she found a corner of the sheet, drew it up, and exposed more of the head wound. "Blood, bone shards, gray matter. Hand me my kit. Looks to me like . . ."

She took the kit, pulled out microgoggles. With them, she leaned in. "Yeah, murder weapon's going to be a crowbar. I can see where the two-pronged hook went in, the flat handle indented."

Gently, Eve turned the head. "Two strikes, right temple, upper back of the head. One probably did it."

"Oh hell. Lieutenant, I know her. Getz?"

He rose up a little, leaned in. "Yeah, shit. Sidewalk sleeper, sir. She roamed around this area, did some unlicensed begging."

"We looked the other way there," Urly added. "She was harmless.

She'd make little flowers or paper animals out of litter, pass them out to anyone who gave her some change, you know?"

"Got a name?"

"No, sir. She used the Chelsea Shelter mostly in the winter or bad weather. Or flopped in one of the condemned buildings here like a lot of them. She didn't hustle or hassle, but she kept a little book, and wrote people up for rule violations."

"What kind of violations?" Eve asked as she got out her Identi-pad.

"Jaywalking, littering—she was fierce about littering—shoplifting, trespassing, not picking up your dog's poop." Urly shrugged. "She'd write down a kind of description of the violator, the violation, the time and place. She'd hunt up a cop and read off the page. Ask us to make a copy."

"Mostly, we would, and we'd thank her, give her a couple bucks," Getz added. "We all called her CC—for Concerned Citizen."

"Spotty on the ID data, lot of blank spots. But she comes up as Alva Quirk, mixed race, age forty-six. No fixed address. No current employment. No family listed on her ID. We'll do a run there."

"Alva," Urly repeated. "Lieutenant, if it turns out she doesn't have family, the cops in the Tenth would take care of having her cremated. She was kind of a mascot."

"I'll make sure you're notified. TOD, zero-one-twenty. COD, blunt and sharp head trauma. ME to confirm."

Eve heard the clomping, recognized pink cowgirl boots. "Peabody," she said without looking up. "Just in time. Everybody, seal up, and let's get her out. I can get her up," Eve said before Getz could climb in with her. "I can get her up and pass her to you."

It was a process, and not a pleasant one, but Eve slid her arms along and under the plastic, got a grip.

Even deadweight, the victim couldn't have been more than a hundred pounds.

Urly reached over, took some of that weight, then Getz and Peabody helped lift the legs.

They laid her, the sheet still wrapped around her lower body, on the ground in front of the dumpster.

Eve crouched down to check the multiple pockets of Alva's faded gray baggies. "No book, no nothing."

"She usually had a backpack, but she kept the book and a pencil in her pocket."

"Not there now." She looked back at the dumpster, thought: Fuck.

She looked up at her partner. It still took her an extra instant to adjust to the red tips and streaks in Peabody's dark, now flippy hair. In fact, Eve thought she registered a few more of both streaks and flips.

"Peabody, Officer Getz is going to take you to the wit who found her. Get his statement. There has to be some security around this site—get copies of any discs or hunt up any security guards. And make sure whoever's in charge knows this site is shut down until I say otherwise."

"I got it."

"Let's open up the rest of this plastic."

When she and Urly unwrapped the lower body, Eve saw the stub of a pencil in the ragged cuff of the baggies.

"Pencil stub, caught in the cuff of her pants," she said for the record as she took out an evidence bag. "Dropped it when she got bashed and it got caught in there. Someone didn't want to be in her book. I'm not going to find the book or her backpack in that dumpster. Gotta look, but the killer took all that. Missed the pencil, but this was a rush job."

She sat back on her heels a moment, because she could see it. "Murder weapon may be in there, but smarter, if they were going to leave it, to wrap it up with her. We're going to find the kill site. Cleaned up some of the blood, but it was dark—even with the security lights, you wouldn't get it all. And he was sloppy, didn't wrap her nice and tight, so she started coming out of the sheeting, dripped some blood.

"Maybe she was flopping here for the night. They've got the buildings locked up, fenced off while they're doing what they do, but it's familiar here, so she comes here for the night. Nice night, who wants to be ass to elbow in a shelter on a nice night? Hears something, sees something. Can't have that, gotta write that down for my police friends."

"Oh crap, Lieutenant, that sounds right."

"Illegals deal, rape, mugging—it's not going to be littering or dog shit. He could take the book, but what's to stop her from telling somebody? Only one way to fix that. Where did he get the crowbar? Because that's what it's going to be."

As she spoke, she ran her hands over the victim, checked for other wounds, offensive, defensive. "Just the two strikes to the head. Back of the head when she'd turned away, right temple on her way down, to make sure. Take the book, the backpack, check her pockets and take whatever she has. Get the sheeting—has to know where to find it— wrap her up, carry her over to the dumpster, drop her in."

"Why not just leave her where she fell?"

"Somebody might come by, find her. You've got to get away, ditch that pack, destroy that book, and clean up. You got blood on you, you got spatter. Nobody's going to find her for hours. Likely a couple hours more than the wit did because of the sloppy."

"She said to me once, she had to take care of New York because New York took care of her."

"That's just what we're going to do, Officer. We're going to take care of her."

Rising, Eve called for the sweepers and for the morgue.

"Stay with the body," she told Urly, then boosted herself back into the dumpster.

Urly gave her that hint of a smile again. "Those are really nice boots."

"Well, they were. Describe the book."

By the time Eve swung out, empty-handed, Peabody was waiting for her.

"The wit just started working for Singer Family Developers, and on this job," Peabody began. "His uncle's one of the crew, got him in for the summer. He saw the blood, thought there was an animal in the dumpster, maybe just hurt, so he took a look. Saw the body and, in his words, 'went freaked.'"

"Did he touch anything?"

"He says no. Too freaked. But he called it in, then tagged his uncle."

Peabody shifted on her pink boots, careful to keep them away from the dried blood.

"The wit was one of the first on the job this morning—trying to make good—and his uncle was just pulling up. Uncle took a look, too, and they waited for Urly and Getz. While they waited, the uncle—Marvin Shellering—contacted the foreman, who contacted Singer. That's Bolton Kincade Singer, who took over from James Bolton Singer, his father, about seven years ago. Singer is cooperating. I've got security discs, but am told they don't cover this area—just the buildings. Nothing back here that needs security according to Paulie Geraldi, the foreman."

Peabody glanced down at Eve's now scarred and filthy boots. "You know, the sweepers would've done that search."

"Yeah, and they're going to do another. I had to see if the killer tossed any of her stuff in there with her. Or the murder weapon. Any human security on-site?"

"Not at this point. They have the fencing, the cams, and right now it's a lot of demo. When they start bringing in new materials, they'll add to security."

"A job this size has more than one boss."

"Right now, it's demo, and that's Geraldi."

"All right." Eve pulled a wipe from her kit to clean her hands. "We're going to fan out, find the kill site. The trail leads that way before it stops—or before she started to drip. I'm leaning toward somewhere along the other side of the security fence line, but out of the lights."

She started along the trail of blood. "We need to run Singer, the foreman, and anyone else who has access inside the fence after hours. We start there and—"

She broke off when a woman—eighteen, maybe twenty—called her name as she ran over the rubble.

T-shirt, Eve noted, jeans, boots, candy-pink hair spilling out of a fielder's cap.

Eve concluded one of the crew, and wondered if someone had found the kill site for her.

"Lieutenant Dallas." Her breath whooshed out; sweat streamed down a pretty face nearly as pink as her hair.

"That's right."

"I recognized you, and you, Detective. You have to come. You have to come right away."

"Where and why?"

She pointed. "A body. There's a body."

Eve gestured behind her. "That body?"

"No, no, no. Manny—um, Manuel Best—told me about the woman, and I'm sorry, but that's how I knew you were right here. And I told Mackie I'd run, I'd run right here and get you."

"You're saying you found another body?"

"I didn't, not exactly. Mackie did. Or some of one, and he said work stopped and call the cops, and I said how you were here, and he said go get you. You have to come."

"Officers! Stay with the victim until the morgue arrives. Secure the scene until the sweepers get here. Where?" she asked the woman.

"We're about a block up."

"Part of this construction site?"

"No, no, it's not part of this. This is Singer Family Developers. We're on Hudson Yards Village, residential and office buildings, a shopping arcade, and a green space."

To save time, Eve left her vehicle; taking a block on foot would be quicker.

"Let's have a name."

"Oh, sorry. I'm Darlie Allen."

"And how do you know my witness?"

"Your . . . oh, you mean Manny. Some of us go for a beer—or a cold otherwise—when we knock off. We just hung out a couple of times since we started. He just started with Singer. And we're, you know, going to go out this weekend. He tagged me about that poor woman. He was really upset. And somebody told him you were in charge, and then when we found the body, I came to find you."

"How'd you find the body?"

"We already demoed the main part of the old building. It was a restaurant. We were jacking up the floor, the old concrete platform. The boss says it's substandard—hell, a good chunk of it had already decayed—so we're taking it all. I was watching because I want to learn how to use the jack, and this big piece broke off, and I could see how they were right about it being a crap job in the first place all that time ago, because there was a lot of hollow, and that's not safe. There's a cellar below—and that's already had some cave-in. And it was in there."

"A body under the concrete? We're talking remains then. Bones?"

"Yeah, but they came from a body. It's not like an animal. I didn't look real close after, because it was sort of awful. But I saw how it was mostly dirt and rotten supports and broken beams under the platform, and the body—remains—that was in a kind of hollow place."

They came to a set of iron steps manned by a security droid. It nodded at Darlie.

"You're cleared, Ms. Allen, Lieutenant Dallas, Detective Peabody."

"It's up on the platform over the old tracks. We're revitalizing what they started before the Urbans, then that got all screwed, so they threw up all this substandard after just to get them up, you know."

"Yeah."

Boots rang on metal.

"It's going to be done right this time. Mackie says we're building an urban jewel, and we're building it to last."

She didn't see a jewel. She saw construction chaos, with a section roped off, and farther north the beginnings of a skeleton that, she assumed, would be one of the residential buildings.

"Who's in charge?"

"Mackie. I'll get him."

"Yeah, do that. But who owns it? Who's in charge of the project?"

"Um. You are."

Eve looked into Darlie's big, puzzled green eyes. And said, "Crap."

Darlie raced off to where a number of people stood around the roped-off area.

"I can tag Roarke," Peabody offered. "He's going to want to know."

"Yeah." Her husband, the owner of almost everything in the universe, would want to know. "We'll see what we've got first. Crap," she said again, and started over as a Black guy who looked like he could curl a couple of the airjacks without breaking a sweat peeled away from the rope and came toward them.

She judged him at about forty, ridiculously handsome, and built like a god in his work jeans, safety vest, and hard hat.

"Jim Mackie, just Mackie's good. I'm the job boss. I had them rope off the section where we found it. Her, I guess."

"Her?"

"Yeah, I'm thinking her because it's them. Sorry. It looks to me like maybe she was a woman. A pregnant woman when it happened, because there's what looks like baby or infant or fetus remains with her. Sorry."

He took off the hat, swiped his arm over his forehead. "That got me shook some. The little, um, skeleton."

"Okay. How about you move your people away from there, and my partner and I will take a look."

"You got it. If you need to go down to her? I gotta fix you into a safety harness. The old stairs collapsed even before we took down the building. I don't trust the supports, and the street-level building below is just as bad—condemned for good reason. This was a shit-ass job. Sorry, sorry. I'm upset."

"Shit-ass jobs upset me, too."

That got a smile. "Heard you were okay. Figured you'd be because the big boss, he's okay. No shit-ass jobs when you do a job for Roarke. You do quality, or you get the boot."

"She's the same," Peabody told him, and earned another smile.

Then he turned around. "Get on away from there, move back. Anybody on Building One, get on back to work."

The way people scrambled told Eve that Mackie did that quality work, and knew how to run a crew. She stepped to the rope.

She didn't know much about building, about concrete and beams and rebar, but even she could see a lot in this section was some sort of filler, more like dirt than stone. And curled in it, about eight feet down, between two crumbling walls, the remains of one adult, one fetus.

Too small to be called a child, she thought, and also curled, likely as it had been inside the womb at the time of death.

"Do you know when this was built—poured—whatever it's called?"

"I do. Not the exact day, but the year: 2024. If the really half-assed records are accurate, late summer, early fall of that year. I expect if there's a better record of it, Roarke can tell you the day, and the hour."

Yes, he would, though he wouldn't have owned it in the late summer of 2024. He wouldn't have been born quite yet, she thought.

But he'd know who had owned it. He'd know the owner; he'd know who developed it. Whatever he didn't know, he'd find out.

"I'll take that harness, Mackie. Peabody, contact DeWinter, get her here."

They'd need the forensic anthropologist, but in the meantime, Eve needed a closer look. Whoever they'd been, they, as much as Alva Quirk, were hers now.

"I'll tag Roarke."

While Mackie sent for a harness, she pulled out her 'link.

Caro, Roarke's admin, answered. "Good morning, Lieutenant."

"Caro, sorry. You need to get him."

Always efficient, Caro merely nodded. "One moment."

As the screen switched to holding blue, Eve considered she'd have gotten exactly the same response in exactly the same tone from Caro whether Roarke sat alone at his desk enjoying a cup of coffee or ran a meeting involving the purchase of Greenland.

She didn't think Roarke could actually buy Greenland, but if he could, if he was planning on it, Caro's response would have been the polite: One moment.

Eve glanced over as Mackie held up a safety harness. "Give me another sec."

She took another couple steps away as Roarke's face filled the screen.

He didn't smile. Not annoyance, she knew, but concern. Those wild blue eyes held steady on hers. Making sure she was in one piece, Eve thought.

"Sorry," she began. "I hope you weren't buying Greenland."

"Not at the moment." Ireland shimmered like morning mists in his voice. "Something's wrong."

"I caught one on my way in, but that one's not the issue. It's the one I caught about a block away from the first. That one's on, or maybe it's under, your Hudson Yards Village project."

"Which part?"

"Ah . . ." She looked back at Mackie. "Which part is this of the project?"

"Right here's the Sky Garden phase."

"Sky Garden. Some restaurant you took down, in the cellar of that. They jacked out the concrete over the old rails, and we've got remains, human remains. Two. What appears to be a female and a fetus. I'm calling DeWinter in to examine and confirm."

"A pregnant woman buried under the platform there?"

"The way it looks from where I'm standing. I can only confirm two human remains, which I further speculate, given the platform was built and poured, according to your job boss, nearly forty years ago, have been there a few decades. Again, DeWinter will take that end of things."

"Bloody hell." He raked a hand through that gorgeous mane of black hair. "I'll be on my way to you within ten minutes."

"Okay. I'm going to have to shut down your project until—"

"Yes, yes, we'll deal with that. I'll be there," he said, and cut her off.

"That'll be fun," she muttered. She looked over at Peabody, who nodded, wound a finger in the air. More fun, Eve thought, with the fashionable Dr. DeWinter coming up.

She stepped back to Mackie, looked at the harness, looked down in the hole. "All right then, let's get me suited up so I can make sure this isn't some sick prank."

Hope lit all over his face. "Oh, hey, like maybe it's fake?"

"I'll know in a minute."

It wasn't, but she had to make that determination even if it meant hanging by a damn cable over a bunch of broken concrete, rebar spikes, rocks, and Christ knew.

"It'll hold ten times your weight," he told her as she put her arms through the straps. "It's got good padding, so it's not going to dig into you, and that adds protection."

He adjusted the straps, checked the safety buckles, the D rings.

"You ever use one of these?" she asked him.

"Yep. I'm not ten times your weight, but I bet I more than double it, and no problemo."

"Good to know."

"DeWinter's on her way." Like Eve, Peabody looked down in the hole. "Do you want me to go down with you?"

"No point. I'm going to get it on record, confirm we've got human remains, and see what I see. I need my field kit."

"We're going to hook it on this ring right here," Mackie told her. "Keep your hands free." He handed her a pair of work gloves. "And protect them. You ever do any rappelling?"

"Not if I can help it." When he laughed, she shrugged. "Yeah, I know the drill. Check in at the other site, Peabody. Start lining up interviews. We need a full run on the victim."

"You're set," Mackie told her. "We'll take it slow. Lot of rubble down there, and where she is, between the walls? That wasn't poured, so it's not going to be real stable."

"Yeah, I see it. Peabody, DeWinter needs to bring recovery equipment."

"She knows."

Of course she knew, Eve thought, and admitted she was stalling.

"Okay." She ducked under the rope, took another careful look so she could mentally map her route down. Then turned her back to it as she pulled on the gloves.

She gripped the belay rope, took up the slack, leaned into it, and started the descent.

Obstacles, she thought, checking left and right behind her as she went down, feet perpendicular to the wall, keeping her pace slow but steady. She adjusted right, left to avoid rubble and rebar and busted beams.

Six feet down, she called up, "I'm moving a couple feet to the left. I can get closer. She's right below those beams, between two walls. Say, how stable do you figure those beams are?"

"They held up so far. We got you, Lieutenant. You're not going anywhere."

While she didn't want to end up somehow breaking through the ground and splatting on the rubble, she'd actually worried more about the remains.

She eased down on a broken beam, gave it a little testing bounce. "Feels solid enough."

Kneeling, she pulled off the work gloves, then resealed her hands. And took a close look at her second and third victims of the morning.

interested in the business, and then was away at college. I do know the buildings went up fast and cheap once the dust cleared."

"Your father sold off a portion of Hudson South-West."

"Yes, years ago. He wanted to build the tower. The Singer Tower. He wanted that signature, you could say, before he retired. He'd hoped to develop the entire project, but he had some health scares. When I took over, I decided there were other areas that took priority. And I wanted that project, where my father had built his signature, to be worthy. It takes time and resources, so I sold the rest of South-West."

"What was Hudson South-West is also being developed now."

Bolton smiled. "I'm aware, Lieutenant. And certain that it will also be worthy. Roarke builds to last, and with the integrity of the city in mind. It's exactly why I approached him about buying the property."

"My partner and I answered a call to that site this morning."

"I'm sorry?" He looked blank for a moment. "But you're . . . You're Homicide. Dear God, not another murder."

"This one, if it proves to be murder, happened a long time ago. The crew found human remains in what had been part of a wine cellar— walled off, perhaps deliberately, to conceal those remains."

"Jesus." His fingers shot through his hair. "How long ago? Do you know who he was?"

"We have to determine that, and will. That, too, will take time. If we date it to when the building itself was being constructed, it would be roughly thirty-seven years."

"Thirty-seven years." More nostalgia, Eve noted, and wistful with it. "I was in college—or just out—and living in Savannah. I didn't want any part of the business back then."

"Why?"

"I wanted to be a rock star." He offered that half smile now. "The troubadour for my generation, like Dylan, like Springsteen." Now he laughed. "More or less. I wanted to write music, to perform. I wanted everything that wasn't my father at that point in my life."

"You left New York to study for it."

"Yeah. I guess you checked. It was about as far away from urban development as it gets. But I know—and I was young and critical—that buildings there, as in other areas, went up hard and fast and cheap. I know some who worked on them weren't . . . there weren't many Paul Geraldis, if you understand me. One of the agreements my father and I made when I said I'd come into the business was the return to our tradition of quality builds. I was very full of myself, even though I'd failed miserably as a performer."

When he shook his head, Eve caught more than self-deprecation in his eyes. She caught just a hint of sadness.

"What was I . . . twenty-four, I guess? My mother appealed to me. Just give it two years. They'd given me four years of college to study my dream. Give the family business two years. So I did, and discovered I could make a difference."

He waved that away. "Sorry, this just took me back. Do you know if this was some sort of accident? A job accident?"

"We don't believe so, but will pursue all avenues."

"I suppose it's not the first time or the last. I hear stories about animal remains, and have heard about human ones as well. The building in Hell's Kitchen you and Roarke transformed into a school. All those poor girls. Was this like that?"

"Something like. Is your father well now?"

"He is. He's needed a few replacement parts, as he puts it. And doesn't appear to take after my grandmother, who's hale and hearty at a hundred and five. His own father, my grandfather, died fairly young. Not as easy to replace parts in his day."

"I may need to speak with him about that development project. He may remember something that would aid in our investigation and identification. Yours is, as you said, a family business," Eve continued. "Would your mother have been involved in the project, or is she involved in your current development?"

"My mother? No, she's never been part of the building or planning. She has excellent taste, a fine eye, so she has, over the years, made suggestions for colors, fabrics, fixtures, furnishings if that applies. But Mom's not one to put on a hard hat and tour a site.

"My grandmother, now," he said before Eve could thank him and stand up. "She was an equal partner with my grandfather, and basically took over when he died. And believe me, she'll still give her opinion, solicited or not, on a project, on details big and minute."

He smiled when he said it. "She's a true matriarch, and shows little sign of slowing down."

"I look forward to speaking with her. I appreciate your time and cooperation, Mr. Singer."

He rose as she did. "I personally, and as head of this company, will help in any way we can."

He walked her to the door, stepped out with her.

"Terry, show Lieutenant Dallas to the small conference room, would you?"

"Yes, sir."

"Let me know if there's anything else I can do. And I'd appreciate notification as soon as we're cleared back on-site."

"You'll be the first."

The small conference room wasn't that small, Eve discovered.

It held a table that would easily fit eight on either side, a massive wall screen, a refreshment station, and a trio of mini data and communication units.

The stone-faced Zelda, on the point of leaving, paused to aim those weird eyes at Terry.

"You're to coordinate, contact the names as Detective Peabody or

Lieutenant Dallas submits them, and have them come here immediately."

"Yes, ma'am."

"Detective Peabody has your 'link code and will contact you. After this initial contact, you can continue to work from your desk."

"Yes, ma'am."

When she walked out, Eve studied the room. "Give us just a minute, Terry. And don't *ma'am* either one of us."

He opened his mouth, closed it, nodded, stepped outside the door.

"She's creepy," Peabody said immediately. "She talks like an authoritarian droid and she has eyes like a snake."

"Yes!" Eve jabbed her finger into Peabody's shoulder. "She has snake eyes. How many have we got?"

"We've got twenty-six who'd have access codes, but only five are in the building today."

"Why? Where are the rest of them?"

"Working on other sites or in outside meetings. Three of those took the early shuttle this morning to a plant near Dayton, Ohio, to check out some man-made stone under consideration."

"Okay, we'll start with what we've got, then round up the others." She checked the time. "I'm going to tag Jenkinson, see what's what, let him know to handle things until I get there. You can send for the first of the six."

"Five."

Eve just gave Peabody a sad look. "Really? You think Snake Woman doesn't have the access codes to one of her boss's pet projects?"

"Well, now I do. The first is Danika Isler, head architect."

"We start there. Do a quick run on her while I tag Jenkinson."

They went through the architect, and Eve eliminated her from the older murder, as she'd have been four at the time, then put her bottom of the list on Alva's because she had a solid alibi up to thirty minutes before TOD, as she and her husband had attended his sister's birthday party in the Bronx, shared a cab on departure just after midnight with two other partygoers, and had arrived home to dismiss the babysitter at around twelve-thirty.

She eliminated the engineer, Bryce Babbott. He'd been sixteen at the estimated year of her unknown victim's death—more than old enough to kill. But he'd lived in Sydney, Australia, until 2049, so unlikely.

"He still has the accent." Peabody lifted and wiggled her shoulders after Eve dismissed him. "Sexy."

"People with sexy accents murder people all the time. He's got two dings for assault—bar fights, but he's not averse to violent behavior. And his alibi for the time in question is that he was home asleep with his current cohab, with his ten-year-old son asleep in the next room. He stays on. We'll take a closer look at him. Who's up?"

"Snake Woman."

"Good. This'll be fun."

"I think she's going to be really pissed."

"That's part of the fun."

Pissed hit the mark.

Zelda marched in, lips tight, jaw set.

"Is there something Terry couldn't handle for you? He's at your disposal."

"Does Terry have access to the Hudson Yards project?"

"Of course not."

"Then we don't need him for this. Have a seat."

"I'm very busy. Accommodating your inquiry has interfered with today's schedule."

"Well, that's too bad. Somebody interfered with the rest of Alva Quirk's life. Have a seat. Or we'll arrange for you to take one in an interview room at Central."

"What for?"

"Let me give you a heads-up. Lying to a police officer during an official investigation can land you in all sorts of . . . difficulties. So you're going to want to be careful when you answer my first question because my partner and I are very good at what we do. It'll be a snap for us to determine if you lie, and if you lie, difficulties. A lot of them."

Eve looked straight into those reptilian eyes. "Do you have access codes to Singer's Hudson Yards project?"

The way Zelda looked at her, Eve half expected to watch the woman's tongue—forked, of course—lash out from between her lips.

"As his admin for the past seven years, I manage Mr. Singer's codes, passwords, swipes—which are routinely changed every two weeks for security purposes."

"That's a yes. Have a seat, and start off by explaining why you didn't put your name on the list of those who had access."

"Because it didn't apply."

Eve could tell the woman wanted to remain standing in a show of defiance and personal power, but she finally sat.

"I manage his security codes, seeing that they rotate, that he has them. I don't *use* them unless he specifically requests that I do."

"Has he ever specifically requested that you access the gates at the project in question?"

"No, he has not, and I have not."

"When's the last time you were at that location?"

"I accompanied Mr. Singer to that particular site in March."

Zelda turned her wrist, tapped at her wrist unit. "March fourteenth, from nine to nine-forty-five A.M. While I do occasionally accompany Mr. Singer to sites if he has need of me, it's more usual for me to work out of this building or from my own home."

"You haven't been at that location since March fourteenth?"

"I have not. Now, is that all?"

Eve glanced over at Peabody, spoke pleasantly. "Hey, Peabody, do you think that's all?"

"No, sir, I don't. We're just going to have to interfere with today's schedule a little bit longer." Peabody held out her PPC, and the ID shot of Alva Quirk.

"Do you know this woman?"

"No." Something changed in her eyes. "No," she repeated.

"Difficulties," Eve said. "Lots of them."

"I don't know her. But . . ." Shifting, she looked closer at the photo. "I saw her. I think . . . She gave me an origami flower."

"When and where?"

"On that day, on March fourteenth. Bolton—Mr. Singer—wanted to see that the security around the buildings to be demoed went up properly. He'd delayed that until as close as he could to warmer weather. The buildings weren't safe, but there were squatters, and he worried they'd have nowhere to go over the winter. He's a good man. He delayed locking that area down as long as he could."

"She was at the site. You and Mr. Singer saw her, spoke to her?"

"No, she was down on the sidewalk. I don't think he saw her. It was cold, and had started to sleet. He insisted I go down, wait in the car while he finished up. He gave me some busywork to do to override my objections. I saw her when I went back down, and yes, used his access code to unlock the security gate we had in place until the area, the unstable buildings were fully secured."

"You spoke to her."

"She was by the gate, and she said we were locking people out, and some people lived up there. I started to just go by her, but she got in front of me. She had this book and a pencil. She said she would have to report me for locking people out because some of them had nowhere else to go."

Back ruler straight, Zelda folded her hands.

"Frankly, I didn't want Mr. Singer to come down and have to

deal with her. He already felt considerable guilt about displacing the squatters. I just told her the buildings weren't safe, they were dangerous, and my boss needed to fix them, to make them safe so no one got hurt. He'd feel responsible if someone got hurt. And, again frankly, if that didn't work, I intended to call the police and have her moved along."

"Did it work?"

"She smiled at me, as I recall, and said that was different. That was being a good citizen. She gave me the paper flower, thanked me, and walked away. She's the one who was killed?"

"Yes."

"I never saw her again. I haven't been back to the site since then."

"What did her book look like?"

"I don't really recall."

"Like a diary? A kid's diary—the paper kind?"

"No." Zelda narrowed her eyes, frowned. "No, not like that. It was more . . . ah, like an autograph book. Like books celebrity watchers carry around to get signatures. Like that, I think."

"Okay. Can you give us your whereabouts from midnight to two A.M. this morning?"

"God, this is absurd. It's intrusive."

"It's routine. Somebody killed her and tossed her in a dumpster like she was garbage. You can deal with some intrusion."

"I had a date," Zelda snapped. "I'm divorced, which if you're even marginally efficient you'd know by this time. I've been divorced for three years, I have no children. I had a date with a man I've seen twice before. We went to dinner, to a club to hear some music. And . . . we're unencumbered adults."

"What time did he leave your place, or you his?"

The faintest, the very faintest of a flush rose up on Zelda's cheeks. "He left just after seven this morning."

"Okay, we'll need the details. Where you had dinner, what club, his name."

Zelda stared straight ahead as she reeled off the data.

"Just to wrap this up, we are marginally efficient, so we know you've worked for this company for thirty years."

"I came on as an entry-level secretarial assistant right out of business school in 2031."

"How did you work up to your current position with the top boss?"

She aimed a withering look at Eve. "I'm good at what I do, and received regular promotions. I was assistant to Ms. Elinor Singer's admin for four years before she formally retired, then I served as Mr. J. B. Singer's admin's assistant for five years before Mr. Bolton Singer, who was at that time vice president, operations, asked me to serve as his admin. I remained in that position when Mr. Bolton Singer took over as CEO."

"Did you work on anything related to the Hudson South-West project?"

Her brow furrowed again. "Yes. The Singers divested themselves of much of that property before I joined the firm, or certainly shortly thereafter. And in my position at that time, I wouldn't have had any part in the larger projects. But I did assist Mr. Singer—Mr. Bolton Singer—with the sale of the remainder of that property to Roarke Industries two years ago."

"Okay. Thanks for your time."

She didn't march out, but she did sort of sail. Eve had to give her credit for it.

"We'll verify her alibi, but that's going to check out. I wonder where Alva kept all her old books."

"Backpack?"

"Depends on how many she had, doesn't it? Something to ponder. Have Terry send in the next."

4

ONCE SHE'D FINISHED WITH THE AVAILABLE INTERVIEWEES, EVE CONSIDERED those remaining on the list.

"See how many of the others we can get to come into Central, and juggle them in."

She got into her car for the drive to the morgue.

"We can split those up, and hit any remaining at home or on a job site." She tapped her fingers on the wheel as she braked at a light. A river of pedestrians flooded across the intersection.

New Yorkers doing the fast-clip dodge and weave; tourists doing the neck-craning goggle shuffle.

Everybody had somewhere to go, she thought. Where had Alva gone? A couple of shelters, maybe Sidewalk City, her little nest in Hudson Yards.

But like everybody had somewhere to go, everybody started somewhere else.

Where had Alva started?

While Peabody worked her 'link setting up more interviews, Eve used her in-dash.

"Search all state records for any and all data on Alva Quirk, female, Caucasian, age forty-six, New York City ID on record in 2048 through 2052, no fixed address, no employment listed."

Acknowledged. Working . . .

It continued to work as she threaded through traffic, parked again. She transferred the search to her PPC.

"I've got the electrician, the IT team—three have access," Peabody told her. "I couldn't tag the head plumber, but I got the foreman on the job site he's working now, and she said she'd have him contact me once he's freed up. That's as far as I got."

Eve considered as they started down the white tunnel. "Find a place, stay on this. I'll take Morris and the victim."

"Works for me."

Eve kept walking, her bootsteps echoing. The lemon-scented chemicals, the air filtration, never quite defeated the underlying scent of death. She wondered why she found visits to the morgue less fraught than stops at hospitals and health centers.

She pushed through the double doors of Chief Medical Examiner Morris's autopsy suite to find him wrist-deep in Alva Quirk's open chest cavity. On his music system, a throaty female voice sang about long, sweet goodbyes.

"I'm a bit delayed on your victim," he told her.

"It's no problem. I appreciate you getting to her this fast. Do you want me to step out? Or come back?"

"No need. Why don't you get yourself a cold drink?"

It reminded her she'd yet to crack the tube of Pepsi from her car, so she went to his friggie, got a fresh one.

As she cracked it, he continued to work.

He wore a suit under his protective cape. She supposed the color was lavender or orchid or whatever they decided to call that palest of pale shades of purple. His shirt bumped that hue up a few more shades, and the precisely knotted tie took it back down again.

He'd braided his midnight-black hair into three sections, then braided those into one, using both shades in the cording. She supposed, like his musical talents, he considered the various ways he styled his hair a creative outlet.

"Do you know how long she was on the streets?" Morris asked her.

"Not yet. Working on that, but at a guess, at least ten or twelve years."

He glanced up, his eyes dark and exotic behind his safety goggles. "She was in remarkably good health considering that length of time. I'd say the fact I've found no signs of illegals or alcohol abuse factors into that. She's a bit underweight, marginally malnourished, but I'd say she made use of free dental clinics and screenings. She never gave birth to a child."

He looked back down at Alva. "She took care of herself as best she could. She has a kind face."

"She passed out paper flowers and animals—made them out of litter. Folded up from flyers and other litter."

"Origami?"

"Yeah, I guess. And she kept record books on people she spotted breaking the law—the rules. Jaywalkers, litterers, street thieves, and so on."

"A concerned citizen."

"That's what the beat cops called her. I'm thinking that's what got her skull caved in."

"Two strikes, and I agree with your on-site. A crowbar."

He switched to microgoggles, gestured for Eve to take a pair from his counter. "You see the indentations from the prongs, how the killer struck downward, then pried out and up. She wouldn't have felt the second blow. She fell forward, bruising her knees as you see, her body rolling slightly before the second strike to the temple. No defensive wounds, no sexual assault.

"But."

Eve frowned. "But?"

"A dozen years or so on the street, you said."

"She's got official data—bare minimum—on record from '48 to '52. A lot of sidewalk sleepers don't update their IDs. It only gets updated if they get pulled in for something, or the shelter they use gets around to it."

"Yes, we see that here often. Take a look at the screen." After ordering it on, he moved to his sink to wash the blood from his sealed hands. "I did the full body scan. You see the damage to the skull, of course."

"Hard to miss."

Eve drank some Pepsi as she studied the internal scan.

"It looks like she had a nose job. Or busted it at some point."

"Yes." Morris reached into his friggie, chose a tube of ginger ale.

"Cheekbone, too. Right cheekbone, a fracture there, not recent."

She understood the "but" now and moved a bit closer.

"Got a pair of fake teeth, lower left." Eyes narrowed, Eve jabbed with her right, hooked with her left. "Broke her right shoulder, right forearm, wrist—both wrists—two fingers right hand, three left. Looks like those fingers were broken more than once over the years. Some of those ribs were cracked. None of it recent, none of those injuries happened in the last weeks or months. Those are old injuries."

She looked back at Morris. "Could've been a bad accident. Vehicular wreck, serious fall, but. Did they happen at the same time?"

"In my opinion the ribs were broken and healed before the injuries to the arm and shoulder. The fingers—and the right index, the left ring finger were broken at least twice, at different times—both before and after the arm and shoulder. Even with your keen eye, you'll be forgiven, as you're not a medical, for missing the slight displacement of the right eye socket."

"Magnify it, will you?"

When he had, she nodded. "Okay, yeah, I see it."

"I estimate the orbital and cheekbone injuries, and the second break on the right index finger, occurred after the others."

"Somebody tuned her up regularly," Eve murmured.

"That would be my initial conclusion."

"How old are they?"

"My analysis, and comp-generated probability, puts them at fifteen to twenty years. But I'd like to send the scans—and if necessary the victim—to Garnet for an expert confirmation."

"Yeah, let's do that. She's already working on one of mine."

"Another?"

"I'll get to that in a minute. I need to . . ." She circled the body, studied it, studied the screen.

"You're not going to be off, or not far off on your estimate. You're too good for that. So that's going to put her in her mid-twenties to early thirties. Not a child, so unlikely parental abuse. More likely a relationship. A spouse or lover."

She held up a finger as her PPC signaled.

"No results, no data on record in the state outside '48 to '52," she told Morris. "Recalibrate search to nationwide and run."

She pocketed her PPC. "Maybe she went rabbit. One too many tune-ups, she goes rabbit. At some point, she wipes her data, or has it wiped so whoever uses her for a punching bag can't find her. But then she puts it back up, or creates a new identity, for these four years. And it takes some skill to fully wipe out official data. Or money to hire the skill. Takes that to create fresh.

"I need an e-man with the skills."

"I suspect you know where to find one."

"Yeah. It'll take time to run the national, then if that comes up zip, a global. I'll get Feeney and his team on it. I'll hit on Roarke for it."

She looked back down at Alva. "It's not going to apply to her murder. I'm not stretching coincidence that she ends up bashed by whoever smacked her around a couple decades ago."

"But you need to know. She deserved the knowing."

"I do. She does. Let DeWinter know this takes priority over the other. For now. Her killer's still out there. For all I know the one or ones who killed my other victims are as dead as they are."

"Victims?"

"Female and apparently a fetus or newborn, remains potentially close to forty years old."

Once she filled him in, Morris took a long pull of ginger ale. "You've had a busy day."

"And it ain't half done. Thanks for the quick work on her. I'm going to find who put her in your house, and as a bonus round, I'm going to track down who beat the crap out of her twenty years ago."

"I trust you will."

When Eve left, Morris walked back to Alva. "We'll all look out for you now."

Eve signaled Peabody to meet her at the car, and considered her options. Rather than tag her former partner and captain of the Electronic Detectives Division, she'd prefer to run it by him face-to-face.

She wanted to set up her board and book—or boards and books, she amended, as she'd been running two cases and three victims.

Still, the remains were in DeWinter's hands now. Until she got something from the bone doc, she had little to do or explore.

When she spotted Peabody, Eve got behind the wheel. Peabody picked up the pace, then slid in.

"I've got everybody but the head plumber, an electrical engineer, two hardscapers, and the security chief. One of the hardscapers is on his honeymoon in Belize, has been for four days. I left a message for the other, who happens to be the groom's sister. The others are on other job sites."

"Good start. I need to talk to Feeney, so if we have any come in before that's done, you take them. Keep it routine, just crossing the t's. We need to evaluate everyone with access."

"You need to talk to Feeney about any potential break in the security at the crime scene?"

"Yeah, that. If there was a breach, what for? Theft, sabotage? Access, it could still be either of those. But it's most likely someone who knew the site, somebody who worked on the site, knew where to get the crowbar, the plastic. But I need to talk to him about the victim. I got stiffed on a regional run on her. National's still in progress. And what Morris found tells me we need an e-man on it."

She filled in Peabody, finishing up as she pulled into the garage at Central.

"It sounds like a hard life," Peabody said as they crossed to the elevators. "And she gave people paper flowers and animals."

"And kept her law-and-order book. I wonder what Mira has to say about those habits. Meanwhile, DeWinter will put Alva at the front of the line."

When the elevator doors opened, the stench rolled out ahead of the occupant. Eve recognized the undercover Illegals detective despite the stringy hair, the scruffy stubble, and the filthy trench over equally filthy baggies.

"Jesus, Fruicki, did you bathe in piss?"

"Pretty much." He grinned, showing blackened teeth. "Got a meet with a Zeus dealer. Somebody's added an extra zing to the street sales. He's my in. Do I look crazy enough for a fix?"

"You smell bad enough."

"Yeah, but that gets me a private ride down."

He shambled off, leaving the fetid odor lingering in the air. Eve eyed the elevator.

"No," she said, turned on her heel, and aimed for the stairs.

"He really looked like a jonesing junkie," Peabody commented as they clanged up.

"He smelled like a corpse covered in cat piss."

She went up two levels, hung a left, and took an elevator from another bank.

It might have been packed with cops, but it smelled normal.

"I'm heading straight up to EDD. Get what you can going, and I'll check in. If you don't need me to take an interview, I'll set up the boards and books. Just keep me in the loop."

"Can and will."

At the first opportunity, Eve slithered out of the elevator to take the glides to EDD. More noise, as voices echoed, but more air to breathe and fewer bodies pushed together.

Then she made the turn into the carnival that was EDD.

Colors clashed and smashed. Patterns streamed and soared. Bold, bright, bewildering. Neon baggies, skin pants, overalls in tones only known to nature in solar systems far away. Zigzags, spirals, lightning bolts, and starbursts.

E-geeks sat in cubes, at desks—always bouncing—or danced along from one point of the big bullpen to the other to the strange music playing in their heads.

She spotted Ian McNab, Peabody's main dish, at his station, skinny hips ticktocking as he stood, tapping fingers on a screen, rainbow airboots shuffling, his head bopping so his long blond tail of hair swung with the movement.

Beyond the usual circus, she got the impression of speed and focus. So something was up.

She headed for the relative sanity of Feeney's office.

He, too, stood, one old brown shoe tapping as he worked a screen. His silver-threaded ginger hair exploded—like a cloud of shock—around his basset hound of a face. His eyes, all cop, focused on the screen.

Unlike those in the bullpen, he wore a suit—the color of dung that had baked a few hours in the hard sun. The knot of his brown tie had gone crooked at the collar of his industrial-beige shirt.

She smelled cop coffee and sugar.

He grunted, stepped back a half step. And spotted her.

"Don't have anything yet. I sent a couple of boys out as soon as I could spare them."

"Okay. You're working a hot one."

He held up three fingers. "We're nearly there with the first—got nearly thirty hours on it, and we've broken through. Second just came in last night. And the third, the big, hit this morning."

He held up a finger, this time as a signal to wait, and stepped over to his AutoChef. "Want coffee?"

She accepted she'd been spoiled, but good coffee, Roarke's blend, waited in her office. So she could wait, too.

"I'm good."

"Spitzer Museum took a hit. It's a small, exclusive joint, Upper East. Privately funded, heavily secured—got all the bells and whistles. And somebody melted right on through, looks like about midnight. Only took one. A painting by that French guy, that Monet guy. Water lilies. Curator said it was insured for a hundred and twenty million. Get that? For a picture of flowers."

Feeney shook his head, slurped some coffee. "Anyway, I couldn't send top tier on your case. We're booking it here to find out how the living fuck they got through enough security it should've slammed shut on a housefly buzzing in."

He slurped more coffee, gave her a long eyeballing over it.

"Jesus, Feeney, you know he wouldn't—"

"Shit, Dallas, I'm not saying that. I'm thinking about maybe tagging him up, seeing if he's got time and room to consult on it."

"That's up to you and Roarke."

"I'm thinking about it. It's a challenge, this here. Pretty slick, pretty fucking smart. I can't say I'm not enjoying it, but Roarke could maybe add to it."

"Was it one of his security systems?"

"No, and that might be their mistake. Who knows? They had it privately designed. It's good, and I'm saying it's goddamn good. Somebody knew his shit to get through it."

"Like maybe one of the designers."

Feeney smiled, full teeth. "Looking there, but we're on the tech. Once we get through the one that's breaking, make a little more headway on the second, I can spare McNab or Callendar for you, for short sprints. You know the kid's spending his off time working with Roarke on a personalized security system for the house Mavis and Leonardo bought."

"Yeah, I knew that. And Peabody's burying me, when she catches me off guard, in tile samples and paint color and Christ knows for their end of the place." Then she shrugged. "It's going to be good for all of them. Anyway, there's no real rush on my e's, not yet. I've got other avenues to work."

"Give me an overview. I need to clear my brain cells for a few."

So saying, he picked up a wonky bowl—his wife's creation—from his desk and offered Eve the candied almonds inside.

Unlike his coffee, his almonds were top-notch. She popped one into her mouth as she started her rundown.

"Looks like we're both looking at inside jobs. You likely have two a few decades apart."

"Yeah, and the Singer business has hooks in both."

And that bugged her. Bugged the crap out of her.

"The guy in charge now, he doesn't give me the buzz, but some hide that really well. He's pretty well covered on the older murder— away at college—and since he owns the place, it's hard to work out why he'd bash somebody for seeing him there. But you've gotta look."

"You've already got the expert consultant, civilian, on the construction angle. Still . . ." Feeney looked back at his screen. "I might give him a tag."

She looked at the screen, and couldn't decipher the figures and symbols. But Roarke could. "He'll have more fun with you. I've got to get going."

She popped another almond on her way out. "Good hunting."

"Back at you," he said, and refocused on the screen.

As she made her way to Homicide, her PPC signaled.

No results, she read on her national search. She tagged Roarke. Feeney could do the same, she thought—and, yeah, Roarke would enjoy the challenge, but she needed an e-man now.

"Lieutenant."

"Yeah, that's me. Listen, I know you're tied up with the Hudson Yards site, but there's nothing much I can do on that one until DeWinter's done her thing. And I had to put my first vic ahead on that. Morris found some old injuries—it looks like regular physical abuse—and I need her to confirm a time line."

"All right."

"Meanwhile I need some e-work, and Feeney's slammed. He's probably going to tag you on the hottest of the three they're working."

"The Monet."

"You know about it?"

He smiled at her. "Not directly. *Water Lilies*, 1916. A brilliant work, and worth well over a hundred million. Double that to a private collector. Wouldn't it be fun to consider how it was done, and who wanted that particular painting?"

He would have once, she thought.

And nobody would have caught him.

"I figured, and what I need's not so much fun. My vic doesn't show up on a national search. She popped up as Alva Quirk for a space of time, but nothing before. No records. So she had them wiped. I figure she got tired of being tuned up, took off, did what she could to go into the wind. I need to find her."

"A thorough washing of official records takes considerable skill or money. Or both."

"You could determine if it's that thorough."

"I could, yes. I've still some scheduling to untangle, and if I understand you, we'll be shut down for several days or more, but for Building One."

"I have to prioritize."

"Understood. Send me what you have on your victim. I'll see what I can do when I can do it. Ah, and Feeney's tagging me now."

"Me, first."

He smiled again. "Darling Eve, you're always first. Now, I do wonder what the NYPSD did without me."

"I look at it this way. We're saving the world from somebody who can steal a dead French guy's flower painting. See you later."

She clicked off, and turned into Homicide.

The only carnival in her bullpen lived in Jenkinson's tie. To her eye, it looked like a sunset on Pluto, after the sun went nova.

She wondered it didn't burn through his shirt.

Deliberately she walked down into her office, retrieved the sunshades she put in a drawer. She slid them on and walked back to the bullpen.

When he saw her, Jenkinson smirked.

"Status."

"Healthy, not close to wealthy, but pretty fucking wise. Baxter and

Trueheart caught a floater—East River. Carmichael and Santiago are in Interview with a suspect on the knifing on Avenue B they caught last night."

He jerked a thumb over his shoulder to where his partner barked into his 'link. "Reineke's running down a lead on the case we caught day before yesterday. We're moving on it. Peabody's in Interview with one of yours."

She scanned the case board as he spoke, nodded. "I'm in my office."

"You got a twofer this morning. If we wrap this up, we can give you a hand if you need it."

"I'll let you know."

In her office, she tossed the sunshades back in the drawer and hit the coffee. She gave herself a moment, just one moment, to stand at her skinny window, fueling up, looking out at the city she'd sworn to protect and serve.

A lot of Alvas out there, she thought. She could have been one of them. Her beatings had started young, ended when she'd been eight and killed the man who'd beat her, raped her, terrified her.

Maybe Alva had killed her abuser. Maybe she'd killed, then run, then tried to vanish.

A hard life, Peabody had said. And a damn hard end to it.

Eve turned away from the window. She set up both sides of her office board. Front for Alva Quirk, back for her unidentified victims.

She sat, started a book for Alva, another for the Jane Doe.

She continued on the book when she heard Peabody's bootsteps.

"Status?"

"I interviewed the security chief. He's clear, Dallas. I was kind of hoping he'd be the link, but he was—and I verified—in Connecticut at his parents' seventy-fifth anniversary party. There's video of a lot of it. He and his husband took a limo to and from because they wanted to be able to drink and stay late. I have the limo company, talked to the driver. He dropped them at home on Third Avenue at zero-two-twenty-two. There's security on their building, and they didn't go out again until they both left at zero-eight-sixteen this morning."

"Okay."

"I want to add he's upset. He'd like clearance to check on the security, find the breach. I told him we were on that. He'd seen Alva around. Not on-site, but on the street."

"We'll clear him when we've cleared the scene. He may spot something, since he's worked it. Feeney's got people on it now. Do you need me on the next?"

"I've got it. It's the IT guy, and he's coming in now."

"If you get a buzz, pull me in."

"I will. I like you're letting me handle this part."

Eve glanced up. "You know what you're doing."

"And I like handling it. I'll go write this one up, take the next."

Eve nodded. Alone, she got more coffee. She put her feet on her desk, studied her board.

Old injuries, a hard life. A believer in rules. Who broke what rule, Alva? Where's your book?

Where's your place? Other books, others breaking rules.

Inside job, she thought again. And a sloppy one. A goddamn unnecessary one. Panic or meanness?

Or both?

More than one killer, almost certainly. No drag marks. Bash her, wrap her up, carry her, dump her.

"I'll find them, Alva," she murmured. "Then I'm going to go back and find who broke you."

Since Peabody had the interviews in hand for the moment, Eve dug into the Singer family. The connection between the two murders on her board ran through them.

The company had its beginnings in the mid-twentieth century, when the current CEO's great-grandfather, James Singer, leveraged a loan—from his father-in-law—to purchase his first rental property: a three-story, sixteen-unit walk-up on the Lower West Side.

James Singer and his son, Robert James Singer, expanded, developed, and built. On his father's death—heart attack—R. J. Singer and his wife, Elinor Bolton Singer, took over the business.

And on R.J.'s death—lung cancer—Elinor Singer ran the company, until she retired and turned the reins over to her son, James Bolton Singer.

Eve brushed through the history, as the founders had been long dead and buried before the Hudson Yards projects. But it gave her a sense. By the time J. B. Singer took over, his family had a solid and expanding business in place.

Under Elinor Singer's lead, and with her son as CFO, they bought the Hudson Yards properties—their biggest acquisition, biggest project not only to that date, she noted, but their biggest development still.

Since construction also began on their watch—with an interruption for the Urban Wars—she took a closer look, beginning with Elinor Bolton Singer.

The daughter of Henry Bolton and Gladys McCain Bolton, she'd grown up wealthy—Park Avenue mansion, and another country home in the Hudson Valley. One brother—and digging there, Eve concluded he'd been groomed for political office before his death in a plane crash. One sister—who'd developed a drug and alcohol habit and died of an overdose at twenty.

Elinor attended Radcliffe, studied business management and finance. Which hadn't helped save her family business, which floundered after her mother's suicide.

Eve made a note to dig into more details later when she could pull the unknown victim's murder into her focus.

Less than a year after her mother's death, Elinor married R. J. Singer and gave birth to J. Bolton Singer, their only child, the following year.

The Bolton financial business went under in the eighties, and Eve made more notes to look into—or hopefully have Roarke translate—what she saw were multiple legal issues.

Upon her father's death following a series of strokes, Elinor sold everything but the Hudson Valley estate. Though it looked to Eve like she'd juggled some of the acreage into Singer for development.

Eve breezed through the society stuff—galas, politics, benefits, fashion—taking away the impression of a woman who'd enjoyed her position, her lifestyle, and knew how to use both.

A widow at sixty, she stepped into the big chair, increased holdings, profits. Maybe a figurehead, Eve thought, maybe not, until she retired.

Interesting.

She lived in her longtime family estate, kept an apartment in the city, maintained a flat in Paris.

Though fully retired for about twenty years, Eve noted she was still listed on the company letterhead as consultant.

J. Bolton Singer was not.

"Did you step aside, J.B., or get tossed?" Eve wondered.

She started to shift to his background when she heard Peabody coming down the hall.

"I think you're going to want in on this interview. I'm getting a buzz—not from her, Chloe Enster, hard- and landscape—but what she's telling me."

Eve programmed her search, rose.

"What's the buzz?" Eve demanded as they walked to Interview.

"It may apply to Singer's partners in the project. Enster says she and her brother saw a couple of people they think are questionable characters on the site."

"I'm always interested in questionable characters."

5

Eve opened the door to Interview. She studied the petite woman in work pants, a scruffy T-shirt, and beat-up boots. She wore her midnight-blue hair in a short braid and studied Eve in turn out of emerald-green eyes that reflected nerves.

Petite she might have been, but she had strong swimmer's shoulders and diamond-cut arms.

Strong enough, Eve thought, to have bashed in a skull with a crowbar.

"Chloe, this is my partner, Lieutenant Dallas."

"Yeah, I got that."

"We appreciate you coming in, Ms. Enster," Eve began. "I'm sure Detective Peabody explained this is routine."

"Easy for you to say." She took a glug from her water bottle. "I know there's somebody dead, and there's a finite number of people who had access to the Singer site. Me and my brother are two of them."

She blew out a breath. "Deke's covered, my brother's covered because he wasn't even in New York last night. But I was, and I got nothing. I busted up with my boyfriend a couple days ago—to be known forever as the Cheating Bastard—and I was home, alone, sulking. I didn't talk to anybody. I didn't want to talk to anybody, especially my friend Lorna, who'd I-told-you-so me to freaking death. Or my mother, because the same."

"All right. Did you know Alva Quirk?"

"That's the woman who's dead, Detective Peabody said. I didn't know her name. But when I saw the picture there"—she gestured to Peabody's folder—"I recognized her. Deke and I saw her up at the site a few times. Early, before the crew. Before they broke ground the first time. Deke told her she wasn't supposed to be up there, how it wasn't really safe. But she said something like it was safe under the stars and gave him like this little origami dog."

Chloe drank again, sighed. "We spotted her little nest when we were doing the early site work, but we let it go. She wasn't hurting anything. I guess if we'd made her leave, kept her out, she'd still be breathing."

"That's not on you unless you killed her."

"I've never hurt anybody in my life. A lie," she said immediately. "I lie. I kicked the Cheating Bastard in the balls when I found out. And once, I punched a drunk who grabbed my ass in a bar. But that's it."

"Both of those sound justified."

Chloe managed a smile. "Felt good, too."

"Detective Peabody told me you saw someone else on the site."

"Yeah." Now she rubbed the back of her neck. "We've done other jobs for Singer, and we did one for Bardov—that's one of the partners on this. Deke and I, we've only been in business four and a half years. We're still building a rep. We keep the overhead down, do the design and prep work ourselves. We've got a tight crew, and pay fair, and we don't cut corners. Quality work for a fair price, that's how you build your rep and your business."

"Okay," Eve said when Chloe paused.

"Okay, well. We did two other, smaller jobs for Singer, and we worked our asses off to get this one. We'd work for them anytime. They pay on time, listen if there's an issue. But we wouldn't do another job for Bardov."

"Because?"

"In construction—like in anything, I guess—some cut those corners. Or know which palms to grease. We did good work for Bardov, but we saw some of that. So unless we're squeezed, we won't bid on their projects.

"This job? It could make us. We didn't know about the partners until we bid, but we wouldn't have backed out anyway. The way we heard it, Bardov's sort of silent partners, and consultants. Singer's in charge of the build. It takes a lot of scratch for a build like this. Most are going to need partners, for the scratch."

"All right."

Chloe shifted. "Okay, so we're up there doing some survey work, and we see a couple of Bardov guys doing a walk-around. This is a few weeks ago, and we saw them by the buildings northwest of the tower. Demo's going on, right, and me and Deke just came back on-site to check some measurements for our design. And the one guy—Tovinski—he's an engineer. We don't get why he's there because we know the engineers on the job, and that's really how we copped to Bardov being more in it than we thought. We dealt with this guy on the job we did for Bardov. He's a corner cutter for sure."

"In what way?"

"He knocks down the quality of the supplies and materials. Right on the edge of it, you know? You're doing a quality job, and you bid fair, then he's pulling down the quality to save more money. We argued it—'cause the cost was in the damn bid, right?—but he went over us. Didn't show on the invoice, get it? But we know what we're working with."

"You're saying this Tovinski padded invoices."

"I'm saying Deke and I know what we're working with, and on the Bardov job we did, what we were working with wasn't what was on the order sheet. It was cheaper grade, down the line."

"Okay."

"And we saw him with a couple of inspectors. Maybe we didn't see him grease the palms, but we sure didn't have any trouble passing any site inspections. And we should have."

Now she shrugged. "It happens, right? The way it is sometimes, but it's not how me and my brother work. And we saw a couple of the Bardov guys on the Singer job—I don't know the names except Tovinski—get into it with a couple of the other subs. Not punch-outs, but it looked close."

"And you think Bardov's company cuts and greases?"

"Well, Lorna—the landscaper and the I-told-you-so pal—said that's what she heard on the job. How they had ties to the Russian mob."

After blowing out a long breath, Chloe took a hit from her water bottle again.

"I don't know from that, but she said she heard it. It could be bullshit. It could all be bullshit, but that nice lady's dead, and somebody did it."

"Do the Bardov people have access—codes and swipes?"

"I don't know. They shouldn't, not at this point in the project anyway, but we're just subcontractors. Just cogs in the wheel, right?"

"Have you heard anything about substandard materials on this job?"

"Not a peep on that. And not on the other two jobs we worked for Singer. But we haven't started our work yet, other than prep, design, ordering. And I only saw Tovinski on-site those two times. We're not on-site much right now, so maybe he's there more."

"Got a first name on Tovinski?"

"No, sorry. We just called him Ivan. He's got the accent and everything."

"Have you worked with Bryce Babbott?"

"Quality," Chloe said instantly. "And . . ." She lifted those strong shoulders, gave them a wiggle. "Frosty supreme. And with Angelica Roost, solid, in my opinion. And Mr. Singer—he takes an interest, knows his ass from his elbow. Not J. B. Singer. We haven't met the old man. We saw the grandmother—she came on-site on both our other jobs a couple of times. Got eyes like a hawk. A little bit scary, if I'm honest, but she gave the work a nod, so we got the second job. Now this one."

"Okay. This is good information. When's your brother due back?"

"A week from Monday. Well, Sunday night, but Monday morning at work."

"We'd like to talk to him. Just see if he remembers anything more than you have."

"Sure. I'll make sure he tags you. I guess you don't know how long we'll be shut down."

"Not yet, no."

"I know you've got to do what you've got to do for the lady who got killed. It's just we put almost all our eggs in this Hudson Yards basket. Biggest job we ever bid on. It's dumping some stress right now."

"As soon as we clear it, we'll let Mr. Singer know. Thanks for coming in."

"I'm all done? You said it wouldn't be too bad," she said to Peabody. "It wasn't." She rose. "Um, you bring murderers and like that in this room?"

"It's a room for interviewing, both suspects and witnesses."

"I can kind of feel them. The bad ones. I'm like half-assed a sensitive. I mostly block it because it creeps me out. But I can sorta feel them."

She shuddered once. "I sure wouldn't want your job."

When Peabody led Chloe out, Eve sat a moment, considering.

Corner cutting, palm greasing. Why not some high-dollar pilfering? She couldn't see how anyone had legitimate business on the site in the middle of the damn night. And being there led to murder.

Tovinski looked like a very good place to start.

She rose when Peabody stepped back in. "Good call bringing me in. It gave me a better sense of her. I'd say a sharp eye and maybe tossing in the half-assed sensitive gives her a solid take on what's going on."

"My father worked construction as a teenager—before he met my mother and started the farm."

"Pre–Free-Ager?"

"I guess he was a half-assed Free-Ager before Mom, but he was always a full-on sensitive. Anyway, he says that some jobs, most jobs, ran clean, and with people having pride in the work. But some, you had that corner cutting, the palm greasing, material walking off the job. And greed ran the show."

"Sounds about right."

"The Bardov company. Do you think they still have ties with the Russian mob?"

"Jesus, Peabody. Yuri Bardov *is* the Russian mob. He's Bardov Construction."

"I've got to catch up."

So did she, Eve thought, because she'd never tangled with Bardov or his crew.

"You hear he's mostly retired. Has to be hitting toward ninety. But maybe he's still got fingers in the pie. Alva sees a midnight bribe going on, or witnesses material walking away, something of the sort, alerts whoever's doing it—because that was her pattern—starts writing in her book and, panicked or pissed off or both, they kill her, dump her."

"And take her book."

"And take her book," Eve agreed. "Write up the interview. I'm going to look into this Tovinski, and take a harder look at Bardov. Didn't have the feel of a mob hit," she said half to herself. "Too damn sloppy."

"I bet Roarke knows the company."

"Yeah, I'm counting on it."

She didn't want to tag him on it right then. She figured he was either catching up on his own work, dealing with the shutdown of his site, or having a little fun helping Feeney in Geek World.

She went back to her office, hit the AC for more coffee, and found Tovinski by using his last name and his employer, the city.

Not Ivan. Alexei.

She studied his ID shot as she generated a hard copy for her board. A hard face, she mused. Sharp and lean, as if any excess had been meticulously whittled away. White-blond hair cut close to the scalp, pale skin, pale blue eyes.

The nephew of Marta Bardova—Yuri Bardov's wife—Tovinski immigrated to the United States in 2023 at the age of fifteen. Now just shy of his fifty-third birthday, he held the title of chief structural engineer for Bardov.

One marriage in 2048—Nadia Bardova, daughter of his uncle-in-law's cousin. Two offspring: son, Mikael, age twelve; daughter, Una, age eight.

Numerous identifying marks in the form of tattoos. Prints and DNA on record.

Juvenile record sealed in Kiev—which meant he had some early bumps.

Adult bumps included three assault charges—and six months inside for the third one—at the age of twenty-four.

Carrying a blade over the legal limit, two counts, ages eighteen and twenty-two. Fines, community service for the second charge. No time served.

Questioned and released over the beating death of a shopkeeper. Questioned and released over the drowning—in a toilet bowl—of a city inspector.

No wits, no physical evidence, suspect alibied.

Nothing since.

"Dead men tell no tales."

"You got that." She stepped away from the body to walk to the window. "We'll get some uniforms to do the canvass, but we're not likely to get a cooperating witness around here. Could luck out, but for a solid ID—a long shot."

She studied the windowsill, angled her head, then put on her goggles again.

"What did you say about the building?"

"It's well maintained."

"Yeah, and these jimmy marks look real fresh. They're faint, careful, but they've scratched the paint a little. And . . . son of a bitch! Son of a bitch. I need tweezers and a small evidence container. The lidded vials, not a bag. I've got a couple bits of fabric. Not so smart as you think, you murdering bastard fuck. Jimmied open the shitty window lock—didn't take much, but you scratched the paint. And when you climbed in, the scratches caught at your pants. Didn't even feel it, just a couple threads."

She drew them out, put them in the container. Still wearing the goggles, she studied them. "But I've got Harvo, the fucking Queen of Hair and Fiber."

She labeled it, initialed it.

"He was waiting for him, that's how he did it. Knows Delgato's routine, so he times it. He was probably leaving by the window about the time we were coming in the damn building. Dell saw Delgato coming in about a half hour before he started banging on the door. Killer grabs Delgato when he comes in, jabs him. No defensive wounds so he's either able to control him or the stuff he put in him takes him out. He's already installed the hook—maybe somebody heard that, we'll check."

She looked up, climbed up, examined the hook. "That's going to hit zero, most likely. It couldn't have taken more than a few seconds to drill through."

She hopped down. "Now he's got time to get the rope ready. No drag marks I can see, so he hauls Delgato up, gets the noose around his neck. He's the one on the chair, not the vic. Stand on the chair, haul on the rope—got some muscle—loop it around the hook, tie it off, good and strong. Step off while he's dangling, knock the chair down, and then leave the way you came. Sealed up—we're not going to find prints, and I'm betting the rope came off a job site, one Delgato worked. I'm betting that."

She glanced toward the door when she heard footsteps. "That's going to be the morgue team. Morris is quick. Go ahead and let them in. I'm calling for sweepers, then we'll do a quick search."

They didn't find any tool for installing the hook. Roarke did locate a fake soup can with a roll of cash. Enough—maybe—to pay a couple weeks' rent. She didn't find his 'link, and that told her she would've found some kind of communication on it to/from his killer.

"No 'link, no appointment book, job schedule, no PPC or tablet."

"You believe, and I'd agree, they went out the window with his killer."

"Yeah. Why risk it? You had to communicate some way or other. And he could have your name listed somewhere."

Roarke looked around again, considered the small, sad life ended there. "And you believe Delgato was responsible for Alva Quirk."

"He was responsible, he was part of it, or he knew who was. Ducked Peabody all day, and damn well told whoever put that noose around his neck the cops wanted to talk to him."

As Roarke did, she scanned the lost-man mess of the single-room flop. "Sweepers won't be much longer, then I'll turn the scene over to them—and they can get the evidence we already collected into the lab tonight. Still . . ."

She looked at Roarke. "That fine dining and bottle of red has to wait."

"I may not be a trained investigator, but I deduced that."

"Sorry. I need to talk to Dell, then I have to go notify the victim's wife. She's still next of kin. And a drop by Bolton Singer's is still on the plate. I can pull Peabody in for all that."

"Why? I'm here, and you don't need either of us for those tasks in any case."

"Partners sometimes hear or see something you don't, or think of a fresh angle."

"Then I'll do my best to be a good partner."

"You already are."

When the sweepers arrived, she and Roarke went down to the lobby. Dell paced the tiny space, literally wringing his hands, while another man, not quite as skinny and clearly a blood relation, sat behind the counter.

"Officer!"

"Lieutenant," Eve corrected.

"Sorry. So sorry. I'm so twisted around. I don't know what to do. We decided we should close to new bookings until . . . We have some week-to-week and month-to-month tenants, but we closed down for now for the rest."

"You don't need to do that, Mr. Dell."

"Told ya," said the man behind the counter.

"My brother, Koby, we're partners—with our cousins. I called Koby. I hope that's okay."

"It's fine. We'll need to seal off 2B. It's a crime scene. We'll clear it as soon as possible. I have a couple officers coming in to canvass—to check and see if anyone saw anything."

"I don't know how I can go in there again. Carmine effing killed himself. I had to get the rent, but I wouldn't have pushed at him so hard if I'd known he'd—"

"Mr. Dell—Jamal—this isn't your fault."

"Told him that, too. Jamal takes everything to heart. He's a GD softie."

"Okay, I'm going to ask. What's with the language censoring? I'm a cop. I've heard it all. I've said it all."

Koby snickered. "Bone-deep habit. Our mama, she won't allow hard language. We said something off when we were kids, we got all heck to pay. No screen time, or no ice cream if that was coming. We got older and slipped? A dollar for every word. You're working and saving your money, you learn. Besides, no telling if she'd hear us where we stand now, even though she lives clear across town."

"Mama's got her ways," Jamal agreed. "I was dogging him on the rent, I can't forget that. I can't forget how I walked right in there and saw him that way. How he got so down he hung himself."

"We haven't determined if he self-terminated."

"But—"

"We're investigating."

"You think it was murder!" Now Koby got up. "That's what you do. Murder."

"She doesn't kill people. She's a police officer!"

"Jamal, you dumb-A. She's the one from the vid, the one who solves murders and stuff. From that vid, *The Icove Agenda*."

"The one with the clones and the murders and that scary business? I didn't watch it," Jamal told Eve. "I watch stuff like that, I don't sleep right."

"No problem."

"He's in it, too." Koby grinned at Roarke. "The rich dude. I saw it twice. It's a solid vid. You guys kick butt. So maybe somebody killed him and made it look like he did it himself?"

"We're investigating," Eve said again. She took out her PPC. "Have you seen this man around? Have you seen him with Mr. Delgato?"

Jamal shook his head. "I can't say I have. But I'm not on the desk twenty-four/seven. We rotate, but even then. We got repairs and such, and we try to get to that right away. And you gotta turn the quick rooms. That's why we have the bell. It'll ping on the 'link of whoever's on the shift. It's mostly me, but not twenty-four/seven."

"He looks mean," Koby added as he studied Tovinski. "A mean white dude, but I don't think I've seen him around."

"I'd like to check with your cousins. You said you rotate."

"Sure. Meesha and Leelo. I can tag them now. Meesha, she's a nurse and works nights right now. Leelo, he's an accountant. He keeps the books."

"Let's do that. And can you tell me when the hook in the ceiling of 2B was installed."

"We never put that in there. I didn't see it. Was there . . . I guess there was. I didn't see, but we never did that to any of the rooms. Carmine must've."

"Or the killer did," Koby said. Darkly.

"Knock that off sideways," his brother ordered. "I won't sleep easy for a month."

"Did Mr. Delgato ever have visitors?"

"He never came in with anybody. Nobody ever came in and asked for him. He was a sad story, miss, ma'am, officer."

"Lieutenant," Eve and Koby said together.

"Sorry. He was sad. His wife gave him the boot, and he said his kids were pissed at him. He worked hard, he said, and he liked to ah, de-stress—by playing the horses. His wife didn't understand. He was a plumber, and he was a good one. I know because I had a toilet break, just bust, and he said he could get me a new one at cost and put it in and all. He did, and it's a fine-looking john, too. Best we got. He said maybe I could take the cost of it off the rent, and the cost of the install, at a discount, off, too. That's what we did."

"I'd like to see that john."

Jamal blinked at her. "You want to see the toilet?"

Koby elbowed him. "She's investigating, numbnuts."

She got the make and model and photo of the toilet, checked with the cousins—no help—and left to do the notification.

"Enterprising, entertaining, and interesting men, the Dell brothers," Roarke commented. "I'll wager their mother is a force."

"I wonder how many dollars she ended up collecting from them over the years. This notification could be messy, especially if you hit the mark, and I think you did, about her still being in love with Delgato."

"I expect it will be. And I expect, when you dig in, you'll find that very fine toilet fell off a Singer supply truck—metaphorically."

"Yeah, he was skimming, helping himself to supplies. And he was helping somebody else do that and more. Enough more it's worth two dead bodies."

Once she'd found a parking spot, and they'd walked a block and a half to the townhome, Eve paused again.

"If she gets sloppy, I need you to be Peabody again. You go soft."

"All right."

"You lean that way anyhow."

As do you, he thought as they walked up to the door, or notifications wouldn't be so hard.

Eve pressed the buzzer.

Angelina had shed her work suit for an oversize tee, leggings, and house skids. She sent Eve a molten glare.

"What now?"

"Could we come in and speak with you?"

"Why? Whatever Carmine's done has nothing to do with me. You see this?" She tapped on the glass of white wine in her hand. "I'm about to drink this halfway decent glass of chardonnay as a reward for a long day, and have a little dinner and relax. Tell him if he needs bailing out to call his bookie."

"Ms. Delgato, it's important we speak with you."

"Then freaking speak so I can drink my damn wine."

"It would be better if we came in."

"Oh for—" She broke off with a hiss, but waved her free arm as she stepped back. "Fine, you're in."

"Could we sit down?"

Angelina arched her eyebrows. "Want some hors d'oeuvres while we're chatting?"

"We'll try not to keep you long. If we could sit down for a moment."

She turned on her heel, marched into the sunny living area with the furnishings done in rich corals and tropical blues. She dropped into a chair, waved again at the sofa and its army of fussy pillows.

"Sit, say it. It took me over twenty-five years to accept Carmine wasn't ever going to change and shut him out of my life. And that's what I'm going to do the minute you're out the door again."

"Ms. Delgato, I regret to inform you Carmine Delgato is dead."

Angelina froze with the wineglass halfway to her mouth. "What are you talking about? You're not even real cops, are you? This is one of his ploys to get me to take him back, and it's just sick." She lurched to her feet. "Get out."

"Ms. Delgato. I'm Lieutenant Dallas with the NYPSD." Eve held up her badge. "You can contact Cop Central and verify my badge number. I know this is difficult, but you're Mr. Delgato's next of kin, and it's my duty to inform you."

"Why did you come here before if you're saying he's dead?"

"We were unaware Mr. Delgato had moved from this address, and wanted to interview him regarding an investigation. When we reached his current address, he did not answer the door, and the building super allowed us entry. Upon entry we found Mr. Delgato hanging from a rope in his apartment."

"You're saying he hanged himself?" Her face went dead white, then instantly, furiously red. "I know you're lying! Carmine would never commit suicide."

"I didn't state he had."

"You just said . . ." Now, breath hitching, Angelina lowered slowly into the chair. "You're saying somebody killed him?"

"We haven't determined self-termination or homicide."

Angelina closed her eyes, held up a hand to stop Eve from continuing. After an obvious struggle for composure, she opened her eyes. She drank half the wine in one gulp, then set the glass aside. Her eyes shined, but the tears didn't fall.

"I can determine it. I knew Carmine half my damn life. He'd never kill himself."

"Why?"

"Because he'd never have what he wanted if he's dead. Do you think this is the first time I booted him? It's not. I always caved and took him back. What he didn't get, would never get, is this time I meant it. I was done. He was never going to change, he'd never keep his promises. But he lived in a place where we'd just circle back, he'd come home, we'd try it all again. He loved me, okay? He loved me, and God knows I loved him. But he loved the horses more. He loved the thrill of betting, of winning, even the punch of losing. Because next time— always a next time with Carmine. No next time when you're dead."

She closed her eyes again, held up a hand again. This time a tear slipped down each cheek. "And hanging himself? Not in a million years."

"Do you know anyone who'd want to harm him?"

She let out a sharp laugh, inhaled a sob. "I told you before, didn't I, he'd get the snot beat out of him now and then. A good ten years ago—after I took him back again—I took control of the money in this household. He got an allowance. That was the deal, one he tried and tried to weasel out of, but I held firm."

She picked up the wine for another, smaller sip.

"A few years later, we go around again. This time I have the house account, but I open my own personal account, I put the investments and this house in my name. Just mine, all of it. That was what he agreed to five years ago to come back. So he'd find people to float him loans. Sometimes he won, plenty he didn't. He'd work side jobs to pay them off, but he got smacked around if he didn't pay them off fast enough.

"He denied all that, but I knew."

"Do you have names?"

She shook her head. Her hand trembled a little as she picked up the wineglass again. "I know his bookie's name's Ralph, but I never met him."

"Has anyone else come here looking for him since you separated?"

She shook her head again. "No one ever came around here. He'd meet them at one of his OTB places, or the track. Or, I don't know, but he knew if that type came around here, it was over."

"He didn't have a computer in his apartment. Did he have a home office here?"

"No. I kept the books, paid the bills. I ran the house. And I kept my office door locked." Two more tears spilled out. "I knew I had to break that cycle, for good. You can't live a good life with a man you can't trust not to steal from you."

She pressed one hand to her mouth; in the other, the wineglass started to tip.

Roarke rose quickly, took it from her. "Ms. Delgato, could I get you a glass of water?"

"Yes. Yes, thank you. It's—"

"I'll find it. Would you like us to contact your children? Would you want your children here with you?"

Now she spread her fingers so her hand covered her face. And just nodded.

When Roarke slipped out, Angelina pressed that hand to her heart. "Where is he? I'm his wife. Whatever he did, I'm his wife. I need to see him."

"He's with the medical examiner. I'll make arrangements for you to see him as soon as possible."

"Because they have to . . . they have to . . . Oh God, Carmine."

"I'm very sorry for your loss. I know this is difficult, but I need to ask a few more questions."

"I don't know who'd do this. Nobody gets paid if you're dead. And he always paid the loans eventually. I'd tell you if I knew. I loved him. I couldn't respect the son of a bitch. I couldn't trust him, but I loved him. I couldn't help it."

"Was he a violent man?"

"Carmine?" She let out that laugh again. "Absolutely not. He was a liar. His addiction made him a liar, an asshole, and worse, but he was gentle and kind. I never knew him to raise his hand to anyone. He couldn't even bring himself to give one of our kids a swat on the butt when they'd earned it."

With her hand over her mouth again, she muffled a sob. "I loved that about him. I loved that sweet, kind, gentle part of him. Hardly ever raised his voice, even when I was shouting at him hard enough to blow the roof off. He didn't have violence in him. No meanness in him. Just that terrible sickness that ate away at everything good."

"You said you couldn't trust him not to steal from you. Would he have stolen from someone else?"

"Not from someone who'd suffer for it, but if he thought, if he'd convinced himself they could afford it, or not miss it? Sure. Because he'd know, you see, he'd just know, that next bet, that next tip on a hot horse? It would bring the rain."

When Roarke brought her water, she sipped it slowly. "I can't do this anymore right now. I was rude to you, and I apologize, but—"

"Don't. Don't, it's not necessary." Eve got to her feet. "Is there anything else we can do for you? Anyone else you want us to contact?"

"No, no. I just want my kids."

"I spoke with your oldest," Roarke told her. "They'll all be here as soon as possible."

"I'm going to leave my card." Eve dug for one. "If you think of anything, please contact me. We'll let you know when you can see him. We'll see ourselves out."

8

When they got back to the car, Roarke laid his hands on Eve's shoulders. "Would you like me to drive?"

"No, I've got it. I still want to talk to Singer." But when they got in, she sat a moment. "It would have been easier, I think, if she'd lost it, just fallen apart, than watching her fight to maintain."

She drew in, let out a breath. "Anyway. She was helpful. Here's what I think."

"Shall I tell you what you think?"

She shot him a look, then bulled out into traffic. "Okay, smart guy, what do I think?"

"You're thinking Delgato didn't kill Alva Quirk, but most likely witnessed the murder. Witnessed it because he was stealing from his employer. Or for his employer—that's to be determined. But stealing, you believe he was, and the one with him—one he was stealing for or who helped him steal—killed her."

"I might be thinking that. As a possible theory."

"And taking it to the next step, you're thinking whoever killed Alva Quirk let himself in Delgato's window, set up what would look like a suicide by hanging, and disposed of the witness."

"You may not have known me half your life, but that's a pretty good take on my current thinking."

"Who says we didn't know each other for half, and more, of another life?"

"Irish woo-woo." But she didn't object when he gave her hand a squeeze.

"So for this next part," she continued, punching it to get through a yellow light, "you'll stick with being Roarke."

"Excellent. I know that role well."

"Singer comes across as a decent sort, but that's not to say he isn't siphoning from the family business, and using a longtime employee with a gambling habit to help. Singer wanted to be a rocker, and he had to give that up to go into the family business. Could be he resents that and figures he's entitled to take what he wants."

"Scars and scabs from shattered dreams." Roarke considered. "If so, as CEO, he could find ways to conceal taking what he pleases."

"And if so, he'd have to have somewhere to put it. Hidden accounts. Or like spending it on a stolen Monet."

"A very fine way to wash ill-gotten funds."

"You'd know, so that's something we'll look into later. For now, I definitely want your take on Singer—and the family if they're around."

"I expect that fine dining and good bottle of red as my reward."

"Sounds fair."

"Perhaps I sold myself too cheap."

That earned a smirk. "That'll be the day."

The Bolton Singers had a double townhome on the Upper East

Side, all rosy red brick and shining windows. It sat on a quiet, tree-lined street where Eve figured the nannies and dog walkers strolled the sidewalks with their charges more than their employers did.

Indeed, as she studied the house, a long-legged girl in a DOG'S BEST FRIEND T-shirt strolled by with a couple of dogs—more like mops with feet—on leashes.

Eve noted that the main entrance, and the door that led to a small grassy area boxed in with flowers and fencing, had cams and palm plates.

She chose the main with its glossy wooden door and pushed the buzzer.

She expected the usual computer inquiry. Instead the door swung open almost immediately.

Youngest son, Eve decided, as he looked early twenties and had his father's eyes. His hair, glossy and brown as the door, curled over his ears and collar in studied disarray.

He had a lean build in worn jeans and tee that asked: SAYS WHO?

Music pumped out of the house as he shot them a dazzling smile.

"Hey, hi. Thought you were Clem."

"No." Eve held up her badge. "Lieutenant Dallas, NYPSD, and Roarke, consultant."

His mouth dropped open for an instant, then he shot a finger at both of them. "Yeah, you are! Frosted! I saw the vid like three times, man. Clones. Up and out! We don't have any here, except I've always wondered about Layla. My sister."

"We're here to speak with your father, if possible."

"Guess it is. We're back there for an after-dinner jam. Clem's supposed to drop by." He gestured them in. "So, come on back."

The house had the feel of a family home, a wealthy one, sure, but lived-in. A lot of space, a lot of quiet colors with slashes of bolder ones. He led them through a sun-splashed living room where matted and framed family photos made up a gallery wall, through another space with a long bar and a fireplace tiled in a cheerful pattern that made her think of Italy.

The music gained volume—drums, a piano, maybe a guitar, something with enough bass to pump against the walls, and a lot of voices.

The tableau in the next room struck as cheerful as the fireplace.

A woman—that would be Lilith Singer, wife—banging it out on the piano, another—middle to late twenties, likely the older daughter, Harmony—beating a serious riff on a set of drums, another man—maybe thirty—standing hipshot as he worked the bass guitar.

Another female with blond-streaked hair curling halfway down her back executed a complicated and complementary series of notes on an electric keyboard.

And Bolton Singer—in jeans as worn as his youngest's—rocking it on a guitar and grinning at a toddler about Bella's age, to Eve's eye, who danced around with her—maybe his—arms waving.

The blend and enthusiasm of the instruments and voices told Eve this was hardly the first time for a post-dinner jam.

The one who'd let them in grabbed a sax and let it wail into the crescendo.

"Now, that's what I'm saying!" Bolton let out a laugh and started to bend down to pick up the kid. And spotted Eve and Roarke.

"Oh yeah, company, Dad."

Every head turned with expressions of curiosity—the friendly sort.

"Kincade, honestly." The woman at the piano shook back her hair—curly like her two youngest children's—with a combination of glossy brown and coppery streaks. She rose, walked toward them with her hand out.

"Roarke. You may not remember, but we met briefly several years ago at a benefit."

"I do, and it's lovely to see you again. I don't believe you've met my wife."

"I haven't, but I'm a fan. Everyone, this is Roarke, and Lieutenant Dallas. Our youngest, Kincade, Layla on keyboards, Harmony on drums, our son-in-law, Justin, on bass guitar, and our dancer, Marvi. Bolt?"

"Sorry. Caught me off guard." He set his guitar on a stand. "Roarke, it's been awhile." He offered his hand before turning to Eve. "You've had a long day, Lieutenant. Why don't we take this in my office?"

"We know what happened. It's all over the media, and we talked about it before dinner." Layla took a step closer to her father, but studied Eve. "Did you find out who did it?"

"The investigation's active and ongoing."

"That's what they always say, right, Justin? Justin's a lawyer."

"Almost." The son-in-law scooped up his daughter.

"I'd say that session worked up some appetites. Let's go have dessert. We'll just give you the room, Bolt." Lilith gave his arm a squeeze. "Come on, gang, that cherry pie à la mode won't eat itself."

The bell rang. "That's got to be Clem."

As Kincade dashed off, his mother called after him, "Bring him back to the kitchen. Sorry for the madness. Why don't I send out some pie and coffee?"

"We're fine," Eve told her. "We'll try not to interrupt any more of your evening than necessary."

Lilith ran a hand down Bolton's arm this time. "Let me know if you need anything."

Eve caught the older daughter starting to object—but so did her mother. It only took a look, and Lilith herded the rest of the family out.

"You have a talented family, Bolton," Roarke began.

"We have a lot of fun. Please, have a seat. You must have questions that couldn't wait."

"Questions and information," Eve agreed. "Carmine Delgato."

"Carmine? Longtime employee. Chief plumber on the Hudson Yards project, and others."

"Were you aware of his gambling problem?"

Bolton sighed. "Yes, of course. I know he's separated from his wife again, and it seems to be sticking this time. I'm sorry about it. The company has offered to give him time off for rehabilitation, but . . . It doesn't affect his work, so we've kept out of his personal business."

He lifted both hands. "Surely you don't think Carmine killed that woman. I can tell you, without hesitation, he'd never hurt anyone."

"That may be, but someone hurt him. He'd dead, Mr. Singer."

"He's . . . My God."

The shock looked genuine. He lost color with it. "Carmine? Dead? Are you saying someone killed him?"

"Unless I'm mistaken, yes. The ME will determine, but I believe his death was staged as a suicide."

"Suicide? Carmine?" Bolton had his hands in his hair like a man who didn't know what to do with them. "That doesn't seem possible."

"Why?"

"He . . . he's an optimist, Lieutenant. Often to his own detriment. He simply believes, absolutely, things will turn around, work out. His long-shot bet would pay off, his wife would take him back. A job that's run into serious problems will be fine with just a little work.

"But why would someone kill Carmine?"

"It's my job to find out. Mr. Singer, you knew Mr. Delgato for a number of years."

"Yes, he worked for us at least twenty years. Twenty-five is closer, I think. I can check."

"In your opinion, was he capable of stealing from the company? He may have thought of it as pilfering, or just skimming a bit here and there."

"No, I don't believe . . ." When he trailed off, Bolton stared over Eve's shoulder.

"You're rethinking the no."

"I . . . He had an addiction, and addictions cause good people to do bad things in the need to feed it. I can say I never suspected him of doing so."

"But you've had material, equipment, go missing from time to time."

"It happens. I'm sure Roarke would tell you the same. We're usually able to track that sort of thing down."

"Have you had that issue on the Hudson Yards site?"

"None that's come to my attention, no."

"On other jobs where he was head plumber?"

"I honestly can't tell you off the top of my head. I'd like to call Harmony in. She's been on parental leave, but she's our CFO. And if you don't object, I'd like my wife here, too. She doesn't work for the company, but she knew Angie, Carmine's wife."

"All right."

"I'll just be a minute." He rose, rubbed a hand over his face. "I'm having some trouble taking this all in. Two people are dead."

Eve watched him walk out. "If he's faking this, he's damn good at it."

"His greatest sin might be using too light a hand with the company he runs. That may be because running it is duty, not passion or even true inclination."

"You have things walk off a job."

"From time to time. And if you let it slide, the ones doing the walking will not only do it again, they'll inevitably up the stakes. So you not only track it down, you let it be known you are. Now and again, things walk right back on—ah, look here, we found the missing items. Just misplaced."

He shrugged. "That's not always the case, of course, but it can and does happen."

"Fuck it. What the hell did you see?"

"As you're aware, we razed what was left of that building, and continued demolition on the concrete, into that cellar because it was unsafe. Substandard materials. That's not unusual, as again you're aware, for post-Urban construction, not for the three years or so before regulations locked back into place. But that inner wall, you see—or I could, Mackie could—it hadn't crumbled as easily or in the same way. It had a different texture to the brick. And while the ceiling above the wine cellar was low-grade preformed concrete, the section, that three-foot section between the brick interior and concrete exterior wall? Top grade, poured and formed on-site to my eye, and Mackie's."

"Done to hide her body."

"These weren't discrepancies we found important prior to finding the bodies. Just idiosyncrasies of the era, the builder, or so we thought. So I took the samples, and as we suspected, everything else used, substandard. But not that single wall, not the span above it. That was built with good, solid brick—very costly at that time—and top-grade mortar, and poured concrete."

"How come she wasn't buried in the concrete?"

"It was formed up, you see, to the exterior wall. And then that section—and only that section—poured, leveled, left to set. The work we could see—as, if you remember from your trip down, that wall wasn't fully down—that was on the sloppy side, with uneven joints, too much mortar or not enough. Not the work, I'd say, of a professional bricklayer or stonemason, but superior material. That single wall."

"Needed it to hold up, willing to spend more—or steal better material—to make sure it would."

"Precisely. You'll have the report, or you can do your own."

"The sweepers would have taken samples. We're not idiots."

"I would never think, much less say, you were. But I could, and did, expedite mine. You have necessary priorities, as does your lab. I wanted to know. The child, Eve. The woman was bad enough, but those tiny bones . . ."

"I want to be pissed. I am pissed, but not as much as I should be, or want to be. Because . . . I went down there, I looked at them up close. Tiny bones," she repeated and had to get up, had to pace.

"It made me think about what's going on inside Mavis, which creeps me out, sure, but . . . It hits cops, too, no matter how long you've been on the job, it hits when it's a kid."

She shook it off, had to shake it off. "I'll bribe Dickhead to push on our analysis. It has to run through the chain, Roarke, to make sure it holds up in court when we have who did it."

"Understood."

"They're not going to get away with it. I don't care if it's Singer's hundred-and-whatever-year-old grandmother who built that wall, I'm tossing whoever put them behind it in a cage."

He smiled a little. "She wouldn't have been a hundred and whatever at the time."

"Don't know how old, exactly, she would have been until DeWinter does her work. But nothing in the background shows she knows any more about laying bricks than I do. Maybe sloppy work, but I'd think more rushed, nervous, had to do it at night, right?"

Hands in her pockets now, she wandered the room. "At night when nobody else is on the site. You can't have a bunch of construction guys around when you're walling up the body of a pregnant woman. Can't have them around when you put bullets into her."

Frowning, she circled around to the other side of her board. "It has to be at night, all of it, the kill, getting the good materials, using them. All the same night.

"Had to put the ceiling in, too, or someone would see her, someone would notice the three feet and a body. They had to have the—what, boards, beams?"

"Support beams—the steel. And joists."

"Those, she falls between them. They hadn't done the floor yet, hadn't cleared all the rock because she fell on rocks. Get the wall up, cover at least that three feet of floor. Doing the form, you said. Forming it up, then pouring the concrete. A lot to do, a lot to do fast."

She stuck her hands in her pockets again. "The floor of the main part—the restaurant part—that was concrete, like the wine cellar."

"The plans were for an industrial look—an upscale industrial ambiance."

"So how do you put that in, form it so you're not just dumping the stuff so it goes down to the lower floor?"

"Supports—those joists—form it out, install the subflooring, the base. Layer the cement over the subfloor. Pour, level, smooth."

"Got it. They didn't have to worry about the rest as long as she was covered, all sides. They could use the other stuff for the rest. Wanted the higher grade for the fucking coffin they put her in."

He walked over to her, slid his arms around her from behind. "And I've pulled your focus away from your priority."

"It's just something I can let simmer around. Plus, I can work it into my interviews tomorrow."

"Let me know when you need the copter to go upstate."

"Yeah, yeah. Now I'm going to write up what I got from Gray, and let all that simmer."

11

Once she accepted she couldn't do anything more until morning, and kept covering the same ground, Eve shut down.

She walked over to the adjoining door to Roarke's office.

He sat at his own command center, hair tied back, jacket off, sleeves rolled to his elbows.

The cat, she noted, had deserted them both, and was unquestionably stretched out across their bed.

"I'm closing up shop," she told him.

He didn't glance up, certainly didn't jolt as she had earlier, but finished whatever he had on his desk screen.

"Without me finding you asleep at your desk or nudging you to give it a rest?"

"You want me back in pissed mode?"

"Not at all. Just pleasantly surprised. I'm happy to close down as well, in just one minute."

"What are you working on?"

"I had some business of my own, then I thought to turn to the fun of sliding into the financials of other people."

"Like who?"

"I've the Singers going in one area, and so far I believe the family has very clever, very enterprising financial managers. Nothing you could deem illegal, just close to a shade of shady, but not over the line.

"So far," he added, and finally looked at her.

"Yuri Bardov, that's another matter. Very complex, very layered— also clever, but I'll wind my way through. A smart, experienced man is Yuri. His wife's nephew isn't quite so smart."

She heard the smug, very clearly. "You've got something on him."

"He apparently thinks that by setting up some of his shell accounts in the Caymans and Russia as well as New York, he doesn't need to bother with all the layers—and what those layers cost—as his uncle does. He also spends lavishly. I can't say if his wife—who lives very well—and their children—who are receiving an excellent private school education—are aware he keeps women."

"Side pieces? Plural?"

"Three, and kept women seems the right term in this case, as he pays for the lovely villa on Corfu for one—along with the minor female child, whose expenses he covers."

"He's got another kid."

"That would be my conclusion, as he transfers funds, monthly, into an account for her education, her clothing, her ballet lessons, and so on."

He leaned back, gestured to the screen, where Eve saw the ID shot of a woman in her early forties and a minor female, age fourteen. "It's the same for the woman in Prague, and the two minors—male and female—whom he supports."

The screen split, showing three more IDs. Adult female, middle thirties, two minors, ages eight and six.

"More recently he opened yet another account after purchasing a home in Vermont for a third woman. Going by medical records she's about thirty weeks pregnant."

Eve studied the next photo. "Busy guy."

"He is, and one who apparently insists on spreading his seed. A man in his position and with his, let's say resources, could easily pressure a woman to terminate a pregnancy—and one would think would use some standard caution to prevent same in the first place."

Hands in her pockets now, Eve rocked back and forth on her heels. All three women, she noted, were dark-eyed brunettes.

So he had a type.

"All of this paid for out of hidden accounts?"

"Hidden, and not very well, and not legal."

"I need to—"

"You'll have it all." Roarke rose as he spoke. "All tidy and clearly drawn in the morning so you can use it as a hammer when you get him in the box."

"It's a really big hammer. No, it's a bunch of hammers. Hidden accounts? Wife doesn't know. Maybe she knows he cats around, but I'm betting she doesn't know her kid has a bunch of half sibs or her husband's shelling out all that money, every month."

"And a very tidy sum it is." Roarke took her hand as they walked, brought it to his lips. "I have to thank you for giving me such an enjoyable task to end a long day."

"I wonder if his uncle knows."

"Now there's a thought. I imagine Bardov might think boys will be boys about the catting about, although one hears he doesn't do the same himself. Never has."

"Is that what one hears?"

"It is. Regardless, those particular accounts aren't set up through the business, or through the financial firm that Bardov uses, and that Tovinski uses for all the rest."

"Where does he get the money for those accounts? All that extra dough?"

At the doorway of their bedroom, Roarke turned her into him. "Aren't you the clever one? And now I wonder if all the funds come from Bardov-sanctioned jobs and tasks."

"Huh." She circled her arms around him. "That makes you a clever one, too. He could be moonlighting so he can pay all that out without his wife, his uncle knowing."

"I'll scratch through more in the morning. Now, why don't we find something enjoyable to end our long day?"

"Yeah." Because she needed it, needed him, she rested her head on his shoulder. "I could use some enjoyable."

In something close to a dance, he circled her to the bed.

Fatigue? Yes, she felt it, knew her energy hit low ebb. But she needed to be held, to be touched, to be loved. She needed to give him the same.

When they reached the bed, he released her weapon harness. She lifted her head from his shoulder as he slid it off.

"How come your shoes didn't get bunged up like my boots, since you went down there?"

"Once a cat burglar."

He toed off his shoes, then eased her back on the bed.

The cat rolled over in visible disgust, then leaped off the bed.

When they lay together, she drew the tie out of his hair so she could comb her fingers through it. "You need to go back to your own stuff tomorrow."

"Is that an order?"

"Like anybody gives you orders. But who's going to buy Lithuania?"

"Lithuania?" He lowered his head to brush his mouth over hers.

"That's a place. Somewhere." Rolling, she reversed their positions, then just turned her cheek to his chest. She could hear his heartbeat, feel it.

It soothed and calmed and helped her believe everything could be all right. At least here. At least now.

Her communicator signaled in her pocket. "Crap. Sorry."

She shifted, dragged it out. "It's good. Uniform Carmichael. They have Alva's books, the medical reports. They're heading back."

She set it aside on the bedside table, added her 'link.

"Now, where were we?"

He sat up, pulled her to him, and took her mouth.

Not calming and soothing, just the here and now.

She let the day, the work, the worries, the rest of the world evaporate with the kiss. And locked herself around him as she answered it with all she had.

He brought her home. Every day, no matter what she faced, he brought her home.

His hands slid up her back, down again. No, not soothing. Possessive. Those long, skilled fingers knew how to take what they wanted, and how to give her what she needed.

She could all but hear him think: Mine. And that, only that, brought a quick thrill that banished fatigue.

Wanting him to share that thrill, she unbuttoned his shirt. Her fingers, quick and determined, shoved the material aside, spread over the hard planes of his chest.

She wanted to touch him; wanted him to feel her touch. Wanted to know his heartbeat quickened with it.

And when he tugged her shirt aside, she pressed against him, skin to skin, so those heartbeats merged.

So right, he thought, the shape of her against him. Long and lean, angular and agile, the tough muscle under soft skin. He yearned for her, endlessly, and here in the dark with the world and all its sorrows shut away, she was only his.

Hands rushed now, yanking at belts. Wanting more.

He thought the *more* they craved from each other, always the more, would never be fully filled. Her body, so familiar to him, remained a source of wonder, and would always be, he knew, if they loved a thousand lifetimes.

He pleased himself, letting his hands roam and possess, his lips taste and feed. And felt her pleasure in that freedom with the rapid kick of her pulse, heard it in her quickened breath.

He drove her up, slowly, steadily, barely clinging to his own control as he sought to shatter hers. When she broke, quaking under him, the thrill of her release spilled from her into him.

Greedy, still greedy, she rolled—cat-quick—to straddle him. Still shuddering, still riding, she took him in. Her body bowed, her head fell back as, swamped in her own needs, she dragged him with her to that edge.

Held him there, held them both in that impossible rush of sensations. So the here and now spun out, spun out, spun out to saturate them both in the desperate rush of joining.

Then with a cry of triumph, when pleasure shook and shattered, she whipped them both over.

She slid down to him like water, once again rested her cheek on his heart. Its wild beat made her lips curve.

"Even better than pie," she murmured, and made him laugh as he shifted her so she could curl against him.

She felt the cat leap back onto the bed, then settle himself against the small of her back.

Sated, sleepy, satisfied, she dropped straight into sleep.

"That's right, *a ghrá*." He brought her hand to his lips to press a kiss to her palm. "Rest that busy brain."

The moon was up, a bright white ball in a starless sky. It spread ghost light over the construction rubble, glinted off the dull metal of the security fence.

Alva, her face bruised, her eyes blackened, swollen, walked beside Eve.

"I liked it here," Alva said. "You can see so far. I wish they hadn't made a fence so nobody could sleep in the apartments, but I still liked it here. I thought I was safe here."

"I'm sorry you weren't."

"Some people are mean." Alva brushed her fingers—crooked, broken—over her bruised face. "Some people are mean. They like to hurt you. Even when you try to be good and do what you're supposed to do, they like to hurt you."

"I know."

"He was supposed to love me." Alva let out a sigh as she looked out at the city, at the lights. "He made a promise to love and cherish me when we got married. He broke his promise. He broke it lots of times. And it broke me."

"You got away from him."

"I don't remember too well because everything hurt, and I was scared, and I couldn't go home because he'd do terrible things to my brother and sister. I'm the oldest. I have to protect them."

"You did." Even in the dream, in the dream she knew was a dream, Eve's heart hurt. "You protected them."

"Nobody protected you, so you know it's important. I ran away, but I had to protect them. Then I was safe, and I learned how to fold paper and make it pretty and sweet."

She offered Eve an origami cat.

FORGOTTEN IN DEATH   169

"Thanks. It's great."

"I liked giving people presents because they'd mostly smile when I did. He found me again, so I had to run again, and I couldn't stop being scared. I had to forget, you know, like you did. I had to forget what came before so I wouldn't be scared all the time. You know."

"Yes, I know."

"Do you think she was scared?"

Eve looked down and saw they stood at the other site, the other scene. That same moonlight washed over the remains below.

"I don't know. I'm going to find out."

"She was going to have a baby, and somebody was mean to her. I'd write it in my book and tell the police, but somebody was mean to me, too."

Eve looked over, saw the blood sliding down over Alva's face.

"I'll find them."

"They've been alone a long time. They should have something." Alva held out cupped hands full of paper flowers.

As she let them fall, they drifted down like little birds. In that strange moonlight, Eve saw those tiny bones move and shift, heard a kind of mewling echo up.

"Baby's crying," Alva said.

With that sound still echoing in her ears, she shot awake.

Roarke sat on the side of the bed, one hand gripping hers while the cat bumped his head against her shoulder.

"I'm okay. I'm okay. Not a nightmare." Still, she couldn't quite catch her breath. "Just a really weird dream."

With her free hand, she stroked Galahad to reassure him. "A little creepy toward the end, I guess. I'm okay."

When Roarke leaned over to press his lips to her brow, like a test, she sat up. "You're already dressed. King-of-the-business-world suit. What time is it?"

"It's half six. I had an early 'link conference."

"Lithuania."

His lips curved, but his eyes stayed watchful on her face.

"Not this time, but I'll be sure to look into it, as you seem to want it. Take a minute, and I'll get us both coffee. You can tell me about this weird, ending-on-creepy dream."

He rose to walk over, open the door to the AutoChef.

"It was one of those deals where you know you're dreaming. You're asleep, but your mind's spinning."

She told him while he again sat on the side of the bed, and she let the coffee jolt her fully awake.

"What does it tell you?"

"Nothing I didn't know. I don't need Alva's books from back then to know what Wicker did, and to follow her from what Allysa Gray told me. I'm working with those elements. And I know—knew—I relate to her on some level because of Richard Troy.

"I think or want to think, or find it's just the most logical conclusion, that she blocked her past out. Maybe deliberately, maybe not. Doesn't apply to her murder anyway."

"And the others?"

"I'm not giving them what they need. Just—well, figuratively—leaving them in a hole in the dark."

"Not at all true." He cupped her chin in his hand for a moment. "Not approaching true. You're prioritizing Alva, which is entirely right, but you're already laying the groundwork for the second investigation. Tell me, would you have passed the second case on if it hadn't been on my property?"

"No. There's no need, at least not at this point. Even though we have a pretty good time line for when she went into that hole, because she fell or was pushed in there, as the trauma to certain bones tell that tale, the science has to catch up."

He was right, she assured herself. But the echo of that tiny, mewling cry haunted her.

"We need confirmation on a date of death," she continued, "her age and anything else DeWinter can pull out of the bones. With luck we get a sketch and a holo simulation of her, and I ID her, go from there. It's in DeWinter's area first."

"Exactly, and still you're talking to and will talk to people who cross both sites. And may have crossed both victims."

Eve looked down into her coffee. "It was the baby crying at the end. It was creepy, and sad."

She blew out a breath, finished the coffee. "Anyway, I need to grab a shower and get started."

"Eve," he said as she started toward the bathroom. "You started the minute you saw the remains. The minute they became yours."

"So did you."

So had he, she thought again as she stepped into the shower. That formed a united front. Whoever had killed, no matter how long ago, would pay. Because they'd never beat that united front.

She let the hot jets pummel the dream out of her, and used her shower time to line up the most efficient order for her day.

When she came out, Roarke sat on the sofa, the wall screen scrolling indecipherable stock reports while he studied his PPC.

The cat sprawled next to him, probably trying to soften Roarke up so he got a shot at whatever was under the warming domes on the table.

Not a chance.

To prove it, Roarke gave Galahad a nudge. "Off you go. You've had your breakfast."

The cat slid down, strolled a few feet away before sitting down to wash. But Eve noted he still had one bicolored eye on the domes.

When Roarke removed them, Eve sat down to a golden omelet, hash browns, and fat berries.

Suspecting spinach hid inside the eggs, she took a careful forkful. Her day started out on an up note when she found nothing but cheese and chunks of ham.

"Good deal."

"I thought you'd earned one."

"I bet you've got a full plate today—besides this one."

"It's an expansive menu. You don't ask me if I've dug up any more on Tovinski because you don't want to add to it."

"You gave me plenty already. I'm going to enjoy sweating him today."

"I'll be sorry to miss that. But the overnight did unearth a few more interesting nuggets."

"Really? Like what?"

"Like transactions into those hidden accounts I told you about. Amounts the search tracked back to the sources, in most cases. The bulk, as one would expect, come from his employer, or investments. Some from his employer are generous—bonuses. But interestingly, in the past thirty-six to forty months or more, there have been others, and in the past eighteen to twenty-four, those amounts have increased. Considerably."

"Others—like individuals? Repeat amounts? Like blackmail?"

"No, though he'd likely insist on cash for an endeavor like that. Individuals, yes, and they repeat, but not the amounts. I'd say the amounts depend on how much material Tovinski can siphon off, or what percentage he charges to switch top grade with cheaper."

"From the Singer project?"

Roarke spread a bit of jam on toast, passed it to Eve.

"Oh, from their Hudson Yards project most definitely. But not only, and not only with projects where Bardov is partnering with Singer. Averaging amounts over these last two years? Tovinski's adding about forty-five thousand a month to his income with his side deals."

"Forty-five," Eve repeated. "A month?"

"For the last couple years, yes. It started off smaller—eight to ten thousand—but it's grown. And I'd say more, as some would be cash deals. The old fell-off-the-truck sort of thing."

Roarke ate some omelet. "I doubt his uncle will be pleased to find out the boy he took under his wing is cheating him."

"He could be following Bardov's orders."

Shaking his head, Roarke lifted his coffee. "I rolled it back to study a few invoices—spot checks, if you will—and the outlay from Bardov's company, accounts received from certain vendors. A jump from there to the individuals who work for or own the companies—then had a quick glance at Tovinski's books—which, again, he didn't hide very well. Not well at all."

"How did you get into all of that? Invoices aren't just laid out there, not without a court order and—"

"Trade secret," he said easily. "You can't use the details of what I've found, of course, but it should be easy enough for a clever woman such as yourself to . . ."

He gestured with his own slice of toast. "Intimate. To, if it helps your cause, give Yuri Bardov a reason to take a look himself. Or to simply make Tovinski sweat harder."

The united front, she realized, already had some cracks along the fault line.

Damn it.

"You weren't authorized to do all that."

"Oh dear." Taking a bite of toast, Roarke looked at Galahad. "She's going to scold me now."

"Hacking into a competitor's books to pull up invoices—"

"Do you see Bardov Construction as my competitor?" He sighed a long, exaggerated sigh. "Well now, that stings a bit."

"Screw that." Part of her wanted to punch him for tantalizing her with data she had no business knowing. "The information's tainted, as it was accessed illegally."

"Technically illegal," he agreed.

Now she wanted to punch him and pull her own hair out. "Bullshit on your 'technically.'"

"It's as innate for you, Lieutenant, to hold that legal line as it is for me to slip a toe over it. Then again, one could argue, if one must, I . . . stumbled upon some of the information while conducting an authorized search."

"Stumble, my ass. When it comes to cyber shit, you wouldn't stumble if somebody shoved you over a trip wire."

"That's sweet of you. We'll say one thing led to another."

She started to snap back, but he held up a hand for peace.

"What I would have told you, through those authorized means, is Tovinski's outlay and expenses far exceed his recorded and legitimate income. Being a clever woman and an experienced investigator, you would wonder where that additional—and considerable—income comes from. I expect you would see about that court order and a forensic accountant."

She ate in silence for a moment because that's exactly what she'd have done. Would do. "You could have kept it at that. Damn it, Roarke, you could've stopped at that. Should have."

"You have me on the could. The should? It's more problematic for me." He looked at her then with eyes calm and clear. "I see a woman who'd escaped from years of beatings and abuse. Who overcame it. And died, brutally, because she never lost her need to do the right thing, to follow the rules."

He rubbed his hand over Eve's. "So, more problematic for me, darling Eve."

Because you see me, Eve thought. And hadn't she seen herself in Alva? How could she blame him for doing the same?

"It's not the same. We both know it's not the same, what happened to her, what happened to me."

"And we both know there are disturbing echoes."

There would always be a few cracks along their line, she decided. It didn't undermine the foundation. Love had pushed him over the line—this time—as much as his own insatiable curiosity.

She couldn't punch him for loving her. Even if part of her still wanted to.

"Forty-five large a month?"

"As I said, he started out with a few thousand here, a few there, and increased it. Last month, he skimmed just over forty-eight thousand."

"Got greedy, got sloppy."

"In this area, he was always sloppy."

"Bardov doesn't know about the women and kids, not all of them anyway, or he'd know about the additional income to cover those expenses. Tovinski keeps banging babies into these women, keeps setting them up with houses and all that. He needs more money."

"It takes balls or stupidity to cheat a man like Bardov."

"He may believe the family connection keeps him safe." Roarke continued to eat. "It won't. I'd have a care letting too much slip to Bardov until you have the nephew sewn up. Otherwise, you're unlikely to find what's left of the body."

"Being a trained investigator, I already figured that."

"And so trained, you'll use that to help push the truth about Alva Quirk and Carmine Delgato out of Tovinski. Being alive in a cage is far better than ending up in pieces and dumped in the Atlantic."

"The sharks took the rest. Classic line," he told her, "from a classic vid."

"I can work with this. But next time—" She cut herself off. "Forget it. Beating my head against the wall of you just gives me a headache." She rose. "I'll contact Reo on my way in, and work it."

Knowing the cat, Roarke covered the breakfast plates so Galahad couldn't lick them clean. "I'll do that."

"Do what?"

"Get your clothes for the day. Your head's already working out what to tell Reo."

"I can think and get clothes."

But he beat her into the closet. "We may get some rain, so you'll want the topper, I'd say. Considering that."

He pulled out stone-gray pants, slim ones, with a strip of leather down the sides. Then a crisp, businessy, mannish white shirt—no frills.

"As you'll have a Russian gangster in your box if all goes your way, we'll go for the vest." Stone gray like the pants, with the back in leather.

"I could've done that."

"Mmm-hmm. Stick with the monotone for the boots and belt—the white shirt keeps it fresh. You'll look efficient, and with your weapon harness, intimidating."

"I am efficient and intimidating."

"Which is why you'll wear the clothes. They won't wear you."

Since it saved her time—and his choice hit simple—she didn't argue.

She heard the crash, recognized the sound of the dome hitting the floor.

Roarke turned on his heel. "Bloody hell."

She snickered as she dressed and her efficient, intimidating, and brilliant husband rushed out to argue with a cat.

Fifteen minutes later, with the cat banished, he walked with her to their adjoining offices.

"Let me know if you decide to go to the Singer and Bardov estates. I'll arrange for the jet-copter."

"I've been thinking I can drive it."

"Eve, the copter can get you there in ten minutes or less as opposed to the ninety you'd need to drive through traffic."

But it would be ninety minutes of annoyance and frustration against ten minutes of abject fear.

"I'll let you know."

When she'd put together a file bag, he took her by the shoulders. Kissed her.

"Depending on the timing, I might be able to pilot you and Peabody myself."

"Can't say yet, but I'll let you know." She kissed him back.

"Do that. And take care of my cop."

"Russian gangsters are just thugs with accents and tats." She started out, paused at the door. "And thanks—sort of—for the lever. Even if I can't use it, I know it, and knowing it, I know him before I sit across from him."

He won't know you, Roarke thought as she left, and again found himself regretting he'd miss that particular meeting.

Her topper lay across the newel post at the bottom of the staircase. Her car waited outside.

It always amazed her.

She texted Peabody.

> Want to stop by the morgue re Delgato. Just meet
> me at the lab. Sent more reports. Read and famil-
> iarize.

As she drove, she tagged Reo. When the assistant prosecuting attorney came on-screen, Eve watched her putting fussy stuff on her eyes.

"Don't you just want to rub the crap out of your eyes once you put that stuff on there?"

"No." Reo gave her image in the mirror a serious study, then started on the second eye.

"I do. I'm sending you files and reports. Alva Quirk."

"Homeless woman. Dumpster. About this time yesterday."

"Yeah, so you got that much."

"We got your report on her identification, yes. You have more?"

"I got a shitload more. I got the sort of more that's going to need a warrant. Alexei Tovinski—nephew of Yuri Bardov's wife."

Reo's hand paused. "The Russian mob killed a homeless woman? Who was she really?"

"Nobody important to them. Also on the dead list is Carmine Delgato—head plumber for Singer. It's all in there, Reo, including Morris's report, the tox report. Look at Tovinski's finances: hidden accounts, lots of women—and children—that aren't his wife. A lot of money that doesn't add up to what he's spending on them. Delgato—gambling issues."

"A little embezzlement going on?"

"You're smart. You'll see it, and get that warrant to take a nice deep dive into his money pile. You're going to be issuing another with his name on it before much longer. For Quirk and for Delgato. And, just maybe, for the unidentified, as yet, woman on the second Hudson Yards site."

"Have you dated the remains?"

"I'm going to see DeWinter. Read the reports. It's a lot, and I'm going to give you more."

"Are you going to make me smile really, really big, and tell me we're going to nail Yuri Bardov?"

"Can't say. Yet."

"I'll start reading, and I'll let you know about the warrant on the financials. How many women?"

"Three—that showed up. Three kids, and another in the hopper."

"Jesus, when does he have time to kill people?"

"You don't find time, Reo. You make it. Later."

Satisfied Reo would come through, Eve tagged Nadine Furst.

Far from the hotshot, camera-ready reporter, bestselling true crime author, and Oscar winner, Nadine answered with a groan.

And dragged the covers over her head in a room lit only by city lights out a window wall.

She said, "Why, God, why?"

"Where the hell are you?" Eve demanded. "Why is it dark? That's not New York out there."

"Because I'm not in New York, I'm in Seattle. I think. And it's the middle of the damn night here."

"Not my fault you're somewhere the Earth hasn't turned toward the sun. I need a favor."

"This is a really bad time to ask me for a favor."

"Do you know any solid reporters in Oklahoma?"

"Why would I know anybody in Oklahoma?" Curiosity, Eve deduced, pushed Nadine's head out of the covers. She frowned, streaky blond hair tangled, foxy eyes heavy, as she held the sheets up over her breasts with one hand. "Why?"

"It has to do with the favor, and a dead homeless woman, the fucker who beat the crap out of her years back in Oklahoma, where he's now chief of police in someplace called Moses."

Nadine rubbed her eyes just the way Eve always wanted to when she had to put stuff on them.

"Did he kill her?"

"No. It's looking like a Russian gangster and the gambling plumber who were embezzling took care of that. But I want the ex-husband, too. That's where you come in. A favor, Nadine."

"Who was she?" Nadine demanded.

Before Eve answered, she heard a rustling, then saw Jake Kincade, rock star and Nadine's bedmate, prop his chin on Nadine's shoulder.

He had purple streaks through his midnight waves, and a sleep crease in his left cheek.

He sent Eve a sleepy smile.

"Hey, Dallas."

"Hey. Ah, sorry to wake you up or interrupt."

"Avenue A had a gig out here," Nadine said, "so . . ."

"And it looks like your workday's starting early, Lois." Jake kissed Nadine's shoulder. "I'll order breakfast."

When he rolled out of bed, Eve had a very clear view of his excellent naked ass backlit by Seattle.

"Huh. Nice," Eve decided as he moved out of frame.

"This feels like a dream. Hold on." The 'link went screen down on the bed. When Nadine snatched it up again, she wore a plushy hotel robe. "What do you need?"

"First, I need you to contact people you can trust, reporters who'll hold on this until I give you the go, and you give it to them. I want it hitting all over hell and back at the same time."

"Seriously, Dallas, who the hell was she?"

"Nadine, she wasn't anybody important. This isn't a big story. He's a cop, and he beat, raped, broke his wife until she got away from him. And he's still a cop, and I need—I want," she corrected, "him to pay. So it's a favor. I want you to help me see that he pays."

"Let me get my notebook."

"Thanks. I mean it. It's not necessary. I'm going to send you everything you need, and you'll know what to do with it. I may not be able to give you the green for a couple days, but—"

"I'll be ready. And I know people I can trust to hold the story. Just give me his name, so I can get myself some background. In Oklahoma? Moses, Oklahoma?"

"Yeah. Garrett Wicker. I'm on my way in. I'll send you what I can when I get to Central. I owe you."

"Hell." On a yawn, Nadine dragged her fingers through her sleep-tousled hair. "It's the middle of the damn night, practically, but I'm going to get breakfast in bed, and I'm going to get laid by a rock star. We can call this a wash."

Relieved, grateful, Eve shoved her way downtown.

12

After a quick stop, she made her way to Morris's double doors. He stood, the protective cape over a suit of molten blue, a pale pink shirt, and a tie that merged both in minute checks.

In one hand, he held a scalpel in preparation, Eve concluded, for making his Y-cut in the young female on his slab.

His music today had a soft voice singing over harp strings.

"I wasn't sure you'd be in yet," Eve said.

"Death doesn't end our day, it starts it. It ended hers at the tender age of twenty-three."

Eve stepped forward. The dead's hair was a tangle of gold with emerald streaks. The body itself was thin to the edge of bony—which made a sharp contrast to the overenthusiastic boob job with the tat of a blue butterfly spreading its wings over the heart.

Eve noted the navel, nose, and eyebrow piercings, the multiple ear piercings.

Under the pale gold tan—no tan lines—the skin read gray.

Blue-and-green polish covered the fingernails in diagonal stripes. On the toes, green on the left foot, blue on the right, with the second toe of each sporting an artfully painted flower.

"Rich," Eve concluded. "Either born that way or she found a generous daddy. The piercings, the tat, the nails, those aren't low-rent or home jobs. Those cost."

She considered.

"Where was she found? What was she wearing?"

"On the floor of her dressing room in her Riverside Drive penthouse—family money. A party dress—just the dress—at about two this morning."

"Going, coming, or at a party?"

"At. Hosting. One of the party guests stumbled over her, and according to his statement thought she was passed out or sleeping."

"Probably because he was as wasted as she was before she OD'd. I'm betting there were lots of illegals and plenty of high-dollar booze at the party."

"You'd win that bet."

"She's been using a long time. Looks like she had an eating disorder on top of it. Her arms are toothpicks, and the faint, circular bruising says ingesting and/or inhaling wasn't doing the job for her anymore. She needed the syringe."

"On the visual, and from the statements, I agree. I'll need to confirm."

She looked at him then. "Why are you on a rich junky's OD? Who is she?"

"The only child of Judge Erin Fester and her former husband, the attorney general of New York. Judge Fester asked for me."

"Fester's solid, and the media will crawl all over this. She knew you'd be respectful and discreet."

"Youth is often tragically foolish. But you're here about your newest victim."

He gestured to his wall of drawers before walking over to open one. "His wife and children are coming in this morning. We'll have him ready."

"You found the paralytic in his system before it had time to dissipate."

"Another sixty to ninety minutes, there wouldn't have been a trace of it. His killer obtained a high-grade, controlled medical substance. Dexachlorine. It's used in conjunction with an anesthetic during surgery so the patient is not only asleep but immobile, which is equally important. Dexachlorine doesn't require a counteragent post-surgery to restore mobility."

"It just goes away."

"In surgery, the anesthesiologist would monitor the patient, administer more if need be. Its effects are immediate but relatively short in duration. Two and a half to three hours at most, depending on the dosage."

"Can't be easy to come by for a layperson."

"If whoever administered it didn't manage to steal it himself, he would have paid dearly for it."

"Or he had a medical source he could lean on, threaten, blackmail. Anyway, your quick work screwed the killer's plans for Delgato to go down as a suicide."

They stood on either side of the drawer tray, with the corpse on it. Eve held out the glossy bakery box.

"And what is that seductive smell?"

"A couple of cinnamon buns. I've got a source."

"I should point out that if you hadn't found Delgato on the line between life and death, it would've been very unlikely for me to find the paralytic.

"But I'm taking the buns."

"If this place runs anything like my department, you'd better have a good place to stash them."

Morris brought the box closer to his nose, inhaled. "I have my ways."

"If I have mine, I'll have Delgato's killer—who damn well killed Alva, too—in a cage by end of shift. Her siblings are probably going to come in for her in the next day or two."

"I saw in your report you'd found next of kin. We'll take care of her until then."

She knew he would, and left him with his soft music and harp strings.

She hit the lab next, and made her way through the cubes, around the counter, by the glass enclosures manned by the lab geeks.

She spotted the head geek's egg-shaped skull as Dick Berenski worked at his station. He hunched, skinny shoulders bent as he slid from one end of his counter to the other on his rolling stool.

Eve walked to the far end, waited while he ran his spider fingers over a keyboard.

"We got your tox back on the hanging guy." He kept tapping, and his voice already sounded aggrieved. "Harvo'll get to your fabric trace when she gets to it. I got drones going through the contents of the dumpster on your other victim. Not going to find squat, but you gotta look. Got her tox back—zip and nada there, like it said in the report. Only blood on her or the tarp's hers. Tarp came from the roll in the storage shed inside the fence on the construction site."

He rolled back in her direction, and Eve saw he was trying to grow a goatee. He'd worked on a mustache once that had resembled a skinny caterpillar with mange.

She doubted this would be any more successful.

"Just because you're stacking 'em up, Dallas, doesn't mean we don't have other cases, other work without your name on it."

Eve said nothing, just held up the bakery box.

His beady eyes went nearly as glossy as the box.

"What's in there?"

Since this was a bribe instead of a gift—they didn't call him Dickhead for nothing—Eve had increased the amount. "A half dozen of the best sticky buns in the city. Possibly the state. Maybe the Eastern Seaboard."

He wet his lips. "Whaddaya want?"

"I had three crime scenes yesterday. The second, unidentified female and fetus."

"Yeah, yeah, DeWinter's got the bones. We got the shoe, some jewelry, bullets. We'll get to them."

"The sweepers sent you samples. Dirt, brick, concrete, block, wood."

"Yeah, yeah, yeah. So?"

"I need a full analysis on the brick from the inner wall, the materials in the outer wall, the ceiling between the inner and outer wall, and the floor and ceiling outside the inner wall."

He gave her a sneer she found severely compromised by the attempted goatee.

"I want a pair of frosty blondes and a pitcher of vodka martinis all served up on a tropical beach. Naked."

She refused to let that terrifying image into her head. "I get the analyses, you get the buns."

She heard Peabody's pink boots clomping her way, but kept her eyes on Dickhead's.

"Lemme see 'em."

She untied the cord, opened the lid a few inches, tilted the box toward him. The scent streamed out, and could have made a grown man cry.

Peabody gave a yip from behind her. "You went to Jacko's!"

Dickhead's long fingers reached; Eve shut the box.

"Did you get any extra?" Peabody all but bounced in her boots. "I'll work out a full hour for half a sticky bun from Jacko's."

"Keep me waiting, Berenski, she gets one and you're down to five."

"Hold on, just hold the hell on." He snatched his station 'link, stabbed at it, rolled a foot away from Eve. "Taver? You got the samples from the Hudson Yards construction site, the Jane Doe remains?"

He slid his eyes toward Eve, hunched his skinny shoulders. "Move it up. That's what I said. Do a quick prelim on—"

"Full and detailed," Eve corrected. "Brick from the inner wall is priority."

He curled his lip at her, but turned away, muttered into the 'link. Then he rolled back. "I've got Taver and Janesy on it. It's going to take awhile."

"Define 'awhile'?"

"Maybe half a day."

"Brick's first. How long for that?"

"Maybe a couple of hours. You said you wanted the whole shot."

"I do." She set the box on his counter. "Don't make me come back here."

"You do, bring me a latte—extra shot!"

Okay, Eve thought as she walked away, she had to give him sarcasm points for that one.

"You let him have the whole box." Peabody sighed, deep, wistful. "Probably for the best. I don't think I have an hour to sweat off that sweet, cinnamony goodness tonight. The decorator's bringing samples. Tile and countertops and cabinets and—"

"I'm taking DeWinter," Eve interrupted. "Go back and see if Harvo's had a chance to start on the fabric traces I got from the Delgato scene."

"Okay. I can't believe you hit another murder after you left Central." Peabody looked up the stairs that led to DeWinter's area. "She probably hasn't had time to do much on the remains."

"Then I'll incentivize her."

"With sticky buns?"

"She's not the bribe-me type. I'll just harass her."

Eve turned, headed up the stairs.

She expected to find DeWinter in her lab in one of her coordinated lab coats using some of her strange equipment on human bones.

She found the bones, the woman's precisely arranged on a worktable and the fetus's on another.

But the only living being in the area sat crossways on a chair, legs dangling over the side while she did something on a tablet.

A kid. DeWinter's kid. Eve knew she had a daughter-type kid.

This one wore bright green high-top kicks, jeans with turned-up cuffs, and a shiny belt with a green tee tucked into them.

Her hair, like DeWinter's when it wasn't sleek and tamed, exploded in dark curls, these with some caramel worked through.

Flower pins scooped it back from her face, a face with skin the color of that caramel with just a dollop of cream.

She turned her head to study Eve out of almond-shaped eyes as green as her kicks.

Eve didn't know much about kids, but she knew when one had a face destined to break hearts. Plus, those eyes. They looked as if they knew entirely too much.

More than an actual human should.

"I know you." She didn't smile when she said it, but swung her legs off the chair to stand. "You're Lieutenant Dallas. My mother worked with you on the Lost Girls—that's what I call them. I read *The Icove Agenda*. They were misguided men who twisted science for their own ends. I'm reading *The Red Horse Legacy* right now."

She tapped the tablet, then set it aside. "I have a lot of questions."

"I've got one. Where's your mother?"

"She had to talk to somebody, but she'll be right back. On the Icove investigation, do you think the clones who got out of the school, most were just kids, do you think they scattered? Or do you think they found a way to regroup, that they found a haven?"

Eve thought of the girl with the infant she'd released herself. Because it wasn't right. None of it had been right. "They've got no reason to cause any trouble or be any threat."

"That's not what I meant." The girl rolled those compelling, far-seeing eyes. "Like I'd be scared of kid clones. There were babies, too. Someone has to take care of them, to feed them, educate them, social-ize them. I feel the Avrils—and it's wrong to take a life, but in a way, a very real way, they were defending their own and others—had a place, a safe place. And a way to help the others."

"I couldn't say."

Now she did smile. "Because you think I'm too young to under-stand. A lot of people make that mistake."

DeWinter's heels clicked toward the lab. "That took longer than I thought. Sweetie, if you want to . . . Dallas."

"Lieutenant Dallas and I were discussing Avril and the clones."

"You'll need to save that for another time, Miranda. The lieutenant has her hands full with her current investigation."

"The woman and the fetus. It's very sad."

Miranda studied the bones with the sad mixed with fascination.

"It's good you have my mother working on finding out who she was, and when and how she was killed. The way you collaborated on the Lost Girls. In that case, the man who'd killed them and hidden their bodies had mental and emotional defects. From what Mom's told me, that doesn't seem to apply here."

DeWinter slid an arm around the girl's shoulders. "I don't think you've met my daughter, Miranda. Her school has a professional day today, and her sitter—"

"Who I don't need."

"Her sitter had to cancel."

"I like coming here. There's so much happening."

"Why don't you go see what's happening with Elsie? She's working on the sketch and holo of the adult victim."

"You want me out of the way while you talk to Lieutenant Dallas."

"Yes." DeWinter bent down, kissed the top of her daughter's head. "Yes, I do."

Miranda tilted her face up. "Can I get a fizzy?"

"Fine. Use my code. And don't wander off downstairs."

The girl rolled her eyes again. "It was nice meeting you," she told Eve. "I'd like to talk to you about the Red Horse investigation when I've finished the book. A lot of people think, and say, there isn't real evil in the world. But there is. I have to decide if I want to work on the science end or the investigative end of stopping evil, and the misguided, and the ones that fall into other areas."

She went back for her tablet, tucked it under her arm. "Did it take you long to learn how to use your service weapon?"

"Miranda."

"All right, all right, I was just wondering. I'm going."

Eve frowned after the girl as she left. "How old is she?"

DeWinter just laughed. "She still wrestles with the dog and bargains for ice cream. But her mind? She's scary smart, and sometimes it exhausts my brain trying to keep up with hers."

"You talk about cases with her?"

"She offers interesting perspectives. I can't shut what I do away from her, so we talk, and I explain. Often that sparks something, shows me another approach." DeWinter's eyes turned cool. "You don't approve?"

Eve lifted a hand for peace. "I don't know anything about kids. She threw me off, that's all. Maybe part of that's because she had the same take I do about the clones. About the Avrils and the rest."

"She wants a happy ending for them. Or at least a just one. I'd imagine you'd hope for the just as well."

"Hope's not enough."

DeWinter nodded as they shifted to the tables. "But it should factor in, shouldn't it? Especially when you're still a child. I can tell you these remains were weeks away from full term, from the chance to be a child. My analysis puts him at thirty-two weeks. Viable, and just over six pounds, and seventeen inches. I found no defects or indications of medical issues. He died inside his mother, cut off from oxygen and nutrition."

"Forty weeks is full term, right?" She knew that from Mavis. "So eight weeks to go."

"Which would have made him premature, but again, viable. He would have lived outside the womb."

"What about the woman?"

"I've only gotten started. Elsie has taken measurements, done a 3D replica of the skull, and is working on the reproduction. I can tell you she was between twenty and twenty-five at TOD. Five feet, six inches in height. We were able to extract DNA, but have just begun an analysis and a search."

"If she went in that hole when the building was going up, that's a long shot on the search."

"We can analyze the DNA, and will. Her injuries, the breaks, the dislocation of the shoulder are consistent with a fall. The damage to the ribs is consistent with gunshot wounds. They recovered three thirty-two-caliber bullets."

"Yeah, I got that report."

"She wore a size seven shoe, narrow. You likely saw that report, and the report that the ring size was a five. It's consistent again with the remains. A delicate build. If she gained normally, given the week of pregnancy, the weight of the fetus, she would have been between a hundred and forty to a hundred and forty-five pounds at TOD. Most likely a hundred and fifteen to a hundred and twenty pre-pregnancy."

"A hair over average height, slim build, small-boned, narrow feet and fingers."

"Long, slender fingers. A bit short-waisted, as she had long legs for her height. The bone structure of the skull? Delicate features. A narrow nose, strong but not prominent cheekbones, a heart-shaped face, wide eyes, well spaced. Her teeth are perfectly even, and while we'll run tests, I found no visible signs of decay."

It didn't give her a name, Eve thought, but it gave her quite a bit.

"So she had dental work—perfectly straight—and good nutrition and hygiene."

"We'll run tests, but yes. I see healthy bones. Nothing to indicate she lived on the street, used illegals. Everything to indicate, at this point, she had good nutrition and good health care, good prenatal care."

"That's helpful."

"I think she would have been very attractive. Early twenties, so on the young side for marriage—if the ring she wore is a wedding ring—and motherhood."

"The jewelry looked like the real deal to me, and the shoe was leather. I'm waiting on those reports, but if they confirm, she had some income or someone who paid for that sort of thing."

"I'll be working on this today, and Elsie will continue with the reproduction."

"Okay, this is a good start. Anything you get, anything, send it to me. I'll take it in bits and pieces."

"You haven't closed your initial case."

"Working up to it."

Eve started out and down. She spotted Peabody just outside Harvo's domain, leaning against the glass wall while she scrolled on her PPC.

"That better be work and not home improvement."

"It is. I skimmed when I got up this morning, but I'm catching up. Harvo had to finish something, but she's on ours now. Jesus, Dallas, we've got Alva's books. We're really going after her fuck of a husband."

"Damn right we are. But he can wait."

She stepped through the doorway.

Harvo looked through a microscope while she tapped her blue-tipped fingers on a mini pad. Over her head, codes and symbols, maybe equations—who knew?—covered a screen.

She wore white baggies and a white sleeveless tee—tame for her, if you discounted the figure of a woman on the back of her shirt flying through what appeared to be a meteor storm above the planet.

She tapped her feet, one, then the other, so her glittery blue toes sparkled through the clear boots.

Blue, Eve assumed, ranked as color of the day, since Harvo had gone for it with her short, spiky hair.

She shifted, swiveled. Eve caught the bold red lettering on the front of the shirt.

GIRL GEEKS SAVE

THE WORLD!

"Yo," she said to Eve as she made an adjustment on the microscope, then tapped something else on the pad.

On-screen the fabric traces popped, magnified. The screen split with the right side full of symbols.

"Sorry I couldn't get anything interesting from your dumpster DB, but I hit solid on the shoe in the wine cellar."

"You took the shoe?"

"Dezi or Coke would've run it usually, but they went and got married. They're honeymooning this week. Anyway, my baby's working on your fabric from the hanging man, but I can give you the lowdown on the shoe."

"What's the lowdown?"

"High-quality Italian leather." She swiveled again, worked a keyboard to bring the shoe on-screen. "European size thirty-seven, narrow, and exceptional workmanship. A classic low-heeled pump in your classic black. Prada."

"Where it was made?"

"No, the designer. It's a designer shoe, and they carried that classic pump, with that heel height and width, that toe shape 2022 to 2025. Before '22, they had a slightly thicker heel, after '25, a thinner with a more narrow toe shape."

"That's good data, Harvo."

"We live to serve. The bad news is, classic black Prada pump. You're never going to narrow down where she bought it if that would apply. Plus, thirty-five, forty years in the deep, dark past."

"It's not the where so much, but the what. Designer shoes, good jewelry. Classic pump. You'd call that . . ."

Harvo arched her eyebrows as Eve gestured to the screen. "Boring, and way, way conservative. Even for back then. A conservative, no-risk, no-statement lady shoe for a lady who could afford a grand for boring shoes."

"A grand. Okay, yeah, it's all giving me a picture."

Something went ding-ding-buzz, and Harvo swiveled back again.

"Okay. First, good eye on the fabric trace, Dallas. You didn't get much, but I don't need much. I could nail it as wool—the good stuff—just eyeballing it."

"Seriously?"

"Sure. How it looks, and the texture. Good wool. Italian again, as it turns out. Very finely combed Italian wool."

"Sounds expensive."

"You betcha. This is ult-grade fabric. And I'm going to give you a ninety percent probability the garment this came from is new. No

"No, no, no. You think I can't see? You think I don't know? You're not my lawyer now. Get out. Get out."

"We'll talk. Alone."

"No. You don't stand for me. You don't represent me. He's not my lawyer now," he said to Eve. "He must leave."

"Sir, Mr. Tovinski has terminated your services, on record. This is his right. I have to ask you to leave the room."

"This is a mistake, Alexei. Take some time," he said as he rose. "Tell them you want time to think, to calm. Do this for yourself. If you contact me, I'll come back."

"Former counsel for Alexei Tovinski exiting Interview. Mr. Tovinski, do you wish to contact different counsel at this time?"

He leaned forward. "We will make a deal. I want a deal."

"Are you waiving your right to legal representation at this time?"

"Fuck the lawyers. We will make a deal. And you will be head of the whole police with what I give you with this deal."

"Well, wow. You must have something really big to offer."

Eve glanced over as Reo came into the room. "And here's handy Assistant Prosecuting Attorney Cher Reo entering Interview. Reo, Tovinski wants to play Let's Make a Deal."

Reo sat, set her briefcase aside. And smiled. "All right, Mr. Tovinski, let's play."

15

"I can offer you anything you could want."

As if fascinated, Reo propped her chin on her fist. "You're going to offer me a villa in Sorrento?"

His lip curled. "You think this is a joke? What I have in here?" He tapped his temple. "With this, you could buy a dozen villas. Now you're only an assistant, but with what I can give comes power, and with power comes money and fame."

He shifted to Peabody. "A young, pretty woman such as yourself has dreams. I can help you reach them. You're three attractive women. You want more than to work all day, every day, taking orders from someone else."

"Goodness, it's like he can see inside our souls." Reo tossed her hair. "Or, no, that's not it, is it, Dallas?"

"No. More like a mirror. Is that how this started, Tovinski? You got tired of taking orders from Uncle Yuri?"

"You don't make the deals." Dismissing Eve, he turned his body toward Reo. "You do. I can give you Yuri Bardov. Think of that."

"Okay, I'm thinking of it. And what do you want in return?"

"I want immunity, full immunity. And I want—"

"No. Do you have a second option?"

"You think we'll play games here?" Voice rising, he banged his fist on the table. "You'll give me what I want, and I'll give you enough for you to take down my uncle and his organization. You're an underling. Your boss will want this."

"The prosecutor's office isn't much interested in Yuri Bardov at this time. While we believe he's a very bad actor, his influence and activities have waned, considerably, over the last several years. He's an old mobster, Mr. Tovinski, who's been more interested in his gardens and fruit trees than expanding his network for quite some time now. We prefer leaving him to the feds."

"Must've been frustrating for you," Eve said. "Always believing you'd inherit this wide, organized criminal enterprise, only to find your uncle slowly getting out of the game. Why take orders from an old man when you could pay him lip service and steal from him?"

"Add the women," Reo put in.

"Oh yeah, the women. Yuri Bardov once may have been a criminal kingpin, but he's remained married—and faithful, according to all agency reports—to his Marta for nearly sixty years. He brought you to America, into his business, treated you like a son because she asked him to. And . . ."

Eve shuffled through her file until she slid out a media photo of Tovinski's wife, his aunt, and another woman in formal dress beaming at the camera. "Your wife is the daughter of your aunt's oldest, closest friend."

"Cheating, stealing, lying?" Reo sighed, then ticked a finger back and forth in the air. "And against family? Uncle Yuri's going to be very upset."

"He knows nothing. He's become a fool. A weak man who forgets what made him great. But there's money, much money in what I know."

Eve glanced at her wrist unit. "By this time, I'm confident in saying he knows everything. Who sent his top mouthpiece to represent you, Alexei? Buy a couple clues."

"He would be disbarred if—"

"They'll both deny it," Reo cut in. "And how are you going to prove Ilyin broke privilege?"

"That'd be a tough one," Eve agreed. "Especially since you'll be dead before the sun comes up tomorrow. He may have stepped back, but he's still Bardov, and you insulted him, betrayed him and your family. You betrayed your wife."

"You can't let him have me killed. You must put me in witness protection."

"You're not a witness," Reo reminded him.

Quickly, he turned to Peabody, held out his hands in appeal.

"He will pay someone to murder me. My own uncle will do this. He's heartless, ruthless. He'll do this because I have too much heart, and I gave it to women not my wife—a wife he chose for me. He'll do this because I wanted to give all my children a good life, and a good life takes money. It was only money, and he has so much. It was for my children, and he'll kill me, and they'll have no father.

"You understand. I can see you have a heart. You have to help me."

"You want me to help you?"

Peabody started to reach her hands toward his. Then she slammed her palms on the table as she lurched up. "You want me to help you? You spineless prick of a slug stain. You greedy, brainless ball of pus. You smashed a harmless, helpless woman's skull in, exploited a desperate addict, then pumped a drug into him so you could string him up without getting your pampered hands dirty."

While Eve watched with pride swelling in her heart, Peabody rounded the table to push her face in his. "How many others have you killed so you could buy your fancy suits and screw around on your wife? You're going down, you whiny asshole fuckwit. We've got you cold, and you're going down. Help you? You bet your miserable murdering ass I'm going to help put you in a cage for the rest of your ugly worthless life."

Eve let the silence hang for a beat. "What she said." Since Peabody's outburst threw him off balance, Eve pushed hard.

"We've got everything we need to put you away for Delgato. Everything we need to prove you used him to help you steal from your uncle's company, Singer's, others. We have what we need to take you down for the murder of Alva Quirk."

Eve leaned back as Peabody came around the table, dropped down in her own chair.

"We know you killed Delgato because you were afraid he'd talk, he'd tell someone how you killed Alva Quirk."

Fear, genuine fear, flickered in Tovinski's eyes before he cut them away.

"You can't prove it. Maybe he killed the old woman. Then himself."

"He couldn't fricking hang himself pumped up with a paralytic, Alexei. Pay attention. You were there. You climbed in the window. Went up the fire escape, went in. Do you think nobody notices some guy in a custom-made suit climbing in a window of a flop?"

She had nothing there, but he didn't know that, she thought. And she watched the idea of a witness strike him.

"We'll be rounding up all your associates and accomplices on your skimming scams and we may be making some deals there, right, Reo?"

"Absolutely. I believe I have the list the forensic accountant so kindly provided." In turn, Reo shuffled through her file. "Yeah, here it is. Small change." She beamed across the table at Tovinski. "I love making deals with small change to rake in the bigger bucks."

"But we don't need them for Alva Quirk. We have her books."

Eve smiled when she said it, continued to improvise as she saw fear bloom.

"Yeah, I figure you trashed the book you grabbed after you smashed Alva's head in. The thing is, she's been keeping those books since she was a kid. She had a hell of a collection. Do you really think the night you killed her was the only time she'd seen you on the Singer site? The only time she'd noted down you were there, where you had no business being?"

"You're lying."

"Test me," Eve invited. "If you live to go to trial, manage to get another lawyer and risk a trial, picture me on the stand reading from one of this sweet, harmless woman's notebooks. Imagine the chief medical examiner describing the killing wounds—back of the skull. Back of the skull, Alexei, and testifying when our APA here shows the crowbar you didn't quite clean thoroughly so it still had traces of her blood and brain matter on it."

"If you put me in prison, I'll be dead. You'll be murderers, the three of you. I want a deal."

"He wants a deal," Eve said to Reo, and Peabody snorted.

"Here's how I see it," Reo began. "We go to trial with evidence so profound I expect the jury would come back with a guilty—all counts—in under an hour. Could be a record. You then spend whatever's left of your life off-planet. We could keep you in isolation—from now and until."

"He'll pay for my death, and my blood will be on your hands."

"How much blood's on yours?" Peabody shot back. "You murdering shitbag."

"Or . . ." Reo let the single syllable sit a moment. "You make a full confession, a full and detailed confession, on both murders, and we immediately transfer you, under another name, to an on-planet facility. You'll be provided with another identity, another background. Think of it as witness protection in prison."

"My children."

"Would Yuri Bardov harm or cause harm to be done to your wife, the women you're supporting, or your children? Lies," Eve added coolly, "cut back on the terms of any deal. Test me," she invited again.

He met Eve's steady gaze for an instant, then shook his head. "No, I have no fear for them. He would never harm a child or the mother who tends them. But I provide for them. I visit them. Children need their father."

"You should've thought of that part before you screwed with your uncle, before you murdered two people to cover that up," Eve said flatly. "You heard the deal. Take it or leave it. Either way, you're spending the rest of your life in a cage. How long a life, and where that cage is, that's up to you."

"I did it for my children. I want the best for my children. The best costs. My uncle, he knows about the oldest in Corfu. He was very angry. Nadia is his goddaughter. He said he would keep this secret as not to hurt her. I would continue to support the child and her mother. It would never happen again. If it happened again, I would no longer be welcomed in his home, I would no longer be part of his family, in any way."

"But it happened again."

"This is my business, not his. It's my private business. I take his orders. He wants me to be an engineer, so I study to become an engineer.

He wants to . . . persuade someone to fall in line. I persuade them. He wants me to marry Nadia, I marry Nadia. I give her a good life. But I have my life, too. He wants to control me, and all the while I see him get weaker, draw back from what made him great. From the man I respected. So I took what I wanted. I took what I needed."

Disgust covered his face. "The man I respected? It wouldn't have been so easy to take from him as I did. He plays with his flowers, his trees. But he still holds the wheel, and won't give it to me. So I took more. What I wanted, what I needed. What I deserved after all the years of doing what he said to do."

"Did he order you to kill?"

He sneered at Eve. "I don't give you that now. Fuck you for that now."

"Move on then. Alva Quirk."

"Crazy old woman with her book and paper flowers. She's nothing. A little mouse in her hole, nothing more. We have business, me and Delgato. To move some material out—we have a buyer, we have the invoices marked as we need. A small shipment, so it's very quick for the buyer to remove and pay and take away."

"Who's the buyer?"

"Fuck you."

"Fine. The invoices and your records tell that tale anyway. What then?"

"We talk, me and Delgato, and arrange for the next shipment, and there she is at the fence with her book. She's sorry, but she has to report us. We broke rules. Delgato goes over, talking to her, talking about how we're just doing our job. He's wasting time, convincing this mouse. I have the crowbar we had to check the shipment, to open the box. I use it."

"You struck her with it?"

"I did what had to be done."

"You struck her with it," Eve repeated. "How many times?"

"Once—no, twice. To be sure. Delgato loses his mind. I think he might faint, he's so weak. I slap him to calm him down. He cries, like a baby, but he does what I say. He gets the plastic and we roll her up, carry her to the dumpster. I take her book—that was before we rolled her in the plastic. I think it should be a day, maybe two, before she's found. And who will care?"

He shrugged that off. Even now, Eve thought, he shrugged off the murder of Alva Quirk like it was only a small inconvenience.

"You were wrong there, on both counts. When did you decide to kill Delgato?"

"Then, but it's not the time, the place, the way. I'm not stupid. He's a miserable man, a weak man, a crying man. I have a source for the Dex—and fuck you on that. I know he'll break. He'll tell his wife, or maybe go to the police, claim he saw it happen, but wasn't part. So I took care of it."

"How?"

"You said how. I took the drill, the syringe, the hook, the rope. His window lock is flimsy."

He flicked a hand in the air. Dismissing it all, Eve decided. Because it had been just another job.

Born to kill.

"He lives in a dump because he's weak and tosses his money away on horse races. I put the hook in the ceiling, make the noose. He's a failure of a man. They will say he killed himself. The Dex only lasts a few hours at most. No one will find him before it's gone. No one should have."

"You've had a real run of bad luck," Peabody commented.

Tovinski ignored her. "When he comes in, I push the syringe to his throat. The bruises should cover the mark."

"You've done this before," Eve said.

"Fuck you on that. His eyes are so wide—he can fear. He knows. I make it quick, and I leave. No one should have found him so soon."

"Okay, let's go over a few details." Eve paged through her file. "Before that, I have another question. Singer, not long after you arrived in the U.S., owned a second site, had started construction. Also Hudson Yards—they called it South-West. It's about a block from the site where you killed Alva Quirk. Did you ever visit or work on that site?"

"My uncle was invested, but he wanted me to get my education, to study the business, yes. But on Bardov projects. We were only invested."

"You never went there?"

He looked genuinely puzzled. "Why would I? If someone there had to be persuaded, or needed a lesson, maybe he would have sent me— like an apprentice. But it wasn't a Bardov project."

"All right. Let's go back over the night you killed Alva Quirk."

When it was done, Eve turned the record off. Two U.S. Marshals came in to escort him out.

"Do you think Bardov will find him?" Peabody wondered. "Or even try?"

"He may try." Reo shrugged. "But I think Tovinski—or whatever name he'll have now—is going to live a very long life in a cell. Only a finite group of people know where he's going, the name he'll have, the background created. And no, I'm not one of them. All I know is my boss and yours signed off on it.

"We did our jobs. The job's done."

"He didn't know about the remains—the woman," Eve said. "I'd've seen it by the time I pushed that. Bardov, maybe, but Tovinski didn't know about it, and he's killed plenty more than Alva and Delgato."

"Let's take our win, Dallas." Reo rose. "We've put a—what was it, Peabody? A spineless prick of a slug stain away, for a couple of lifetimes."

"I'm taking it. I liked the 'whiny asshole fuckwit' myself. Good job, Peabody."

"It felt good."

"Let's write it up, close it out. We'll take Bardov and the elder Singers tomorrow. Let's see if we can pry out anything on our Jane Doe."

In her office, she studied the board before she sat at her desk.

She contacted Alva's brother.

"Detective Elliot, it's Lieutenant Dallas. I wanted to inform you that we've apprehended the person responsible for your sister's death."

She told him what she could, then contacted Angelina Delgato and did the same.

She closed the book, cleared the board. She sealed and labeled the box holding the case files. Instead of calling to have them taken to storage, she lifted the box.

A walk, she thought, just walking it all down herself felt like putting an end to it. And taking a breath.

As she walked out to the bullpen, Yuri Bardov walked in with what she assumed was his bodyguard.

He'd gone a little soft in the middle and carried some extra weight there under a fine suit of apricot linen. The bow tie made him look like someone's dapper grandfather—especially if you didn't know he'd run a murderous and merciless criminal empire for a number of decades.

His hair had gone to silver, and he kept it cropped close. He offered a charming smile. His eyes were as cold as January.

"Ah, Lieutenant Eve Dallas." His voice held only the barest trace of an accent, and came rich and full. "I recognize you. What a treat to meet you in person. I'm Yuri Bardov."

"I know who you are." She stepped over to set the box on Peabody's desk in a bullpen that had gone silent. "I'm wondering if this is the first time you've walked into a cop shop voluntarily."

Those eyes, ice blue, bored into her for five thrumming seconds. Then they brightened as he laughed as though he meant it.

"Just as I expected. You don't disappoint, Lieutenant. I was told, after our very thorough scanning, to address any inquiries I had about my nephew to you. It seems Alexei's gotten himself into some trouble. I'm hoping he's allowed visitation so I can speak with him."

"Peabody," Eve said without taking her eyes off Bardov or his companion. "See about a conference room."

"Yes, sir."

"I hate to take up any of your valuable time."

"You've gone to the trouble to come in, I can spare the time."

"We have room one," Peabody told her.

"Want any backup, boss?"

She glanced over at Jenkinson, who was currently sending Bardov the hard eye. She did her best not to react to a tie swirling with a series of rainbows that might arc across the sky after a nuclear disaster.

"We're fine, Detective. This way, Mr. Bardov."

She took the lead and caught a whiff of Bardov's aftershave. Something citrusy that suited the butter-yellow bow tie.

"May I say, Lieutenant, how I'm looking forward to Ms. Furst's new book and reading about your exploits. A terrifying time that was. My wife and I, and some of the family, were in Europe during that episode. I can confess, I was grateful to be an ocean away from New York."

"Right." She opened the door to conference room one. "Have a seat." She glanced at Peabody.

"Would you like some coffee?" Peabody asked. "Tea?"

"I would love some coffee, extra cream. No tattling, Roger," he said to the bodyguard, who cracked the faintest of smiles. "My Marta is doing her best to wean me off caffeine."

He took a seat—the head of the table—and Roger stood at parade rest behind him.

"My wife, my Marta, is very upset about Alexei," he continued. "Her sister's boy, you see, and like a son to both of us. Dima—that is, Mr. Ilyin—would only tell me Alexei dismissed him. Very rash. I'd very much like to speak with him and make sure he's properly represented.

"Ah, thank you," he added as Peabody set the coffee on the table. After one sip, he laughed again. "Some things don't change. Police house coffee is dreadful. And yet . . ." He took another sip. "Still coffee. Now, about Alexei."

"Alexei Tovinski was charged and has confessed to the murders of Alva Quirk and Carmine Delgato."

"I must insist on seeing and speaking to him immediately. I'm his family."

"You can insist, but you won't see or speak with him. Mr. Tovinski, on record, signed a deal with the prosecutor's office, by this time will have been arraigned and sentenced and transferred to the prison where he'll remain, without possibility of parole, for the rest of his life. Times two, consecutive."

"Under duress a man might agree to anything."

"The only duress he may have felt came from your direction, Mr. Bardov, and his fear you would take action to punish him for systematically stealing from your construction company, your partners."

"You expect me to believe that Alexei, a man as close to me as a son, would steal from me?" He waved a hand in the air—a calloused hand, Eve noted. A working hand. "You're mistaken, and if there is action—legal action—it will be taken against you."

"I'm assuming a man of your contacts and experience would have verified the facts by now. You trusted him; he betrayed you. And killed to cover it up. He betrayed his wife and stole to keep the other women and children secret."

She leaned forward a little. "If he'd rolled on you, if he'd given us anything on you, trust me, Mr. Bardov, you'd be in cuffs right now."

"You're a bold one," Bardov stated.

"I'm a cop. We're the cops that took the man who betrayed you, betrayed his wife, stole from you, stole from your partners, and killed two people so he could keep on doing it."

"You ask me to believe terrible things about a cherished member of my family."

"You already believe it. You know it or you wouldn't be here now. You wanted a last look at him, a last word. You won't get them. He's out of your reach—and you'll find that's solid truth. We made sure of it because death is too easy. It's the end. He's going to pay for a very long time. That's justice."

He studied her as he drank more coffee. "Perhaps we view justice differently."

"No doubt. He refused to implicate you in any crime or illegal activity. Take that for what it's worth. He worried about the other children and their mothers. How they would get by."

"The children are family, however they came to be. Their mothers are their mothers. They will be supported properly."

He paused a moment, frowned into his coffee. "I wasn't aware before this time he had killed the woman, the homeless woman. You may think what you think, but I don't approve."

"What about a young woman, a young pregnant woman at another time, in another place?"

His shoulders drew back, and that cold look in his eyes went fierce. "Are you saying Alexei took such a life? For money? To hide his thievery?"

"Someone did."

"I?" He tapped a fisted hand to his chest. "A woman with child is sacred. Sacred. For all my many sins, as you would see them, this is one I would never, never commit. The life that holds life? Sacred. What does this have to do with me?"

"Another time, another place," Eve repeated. "You can waste your time, money, and resources trying to find Tovinski, seeking your sort of justice. Even I don't know where the cage he'll stay locked in is, but I do know I'll hear if he meets a fatal accident, or gets himself shanked. I'll hear, then, as much as I think he's scum, he'll be mine. And I'll come for you."

"A bold one," he repeated.

"He fears you, and that fear will live in him every day, every night. He'll never stop looking for your revenge. I think that's plenty of justice, even your kind."

"You may be right." He set the coffee aside. "I'm older than I was. I take pleasure in simpler things than I once did. And as the years accumulate, I have less to prove."

He got to his feet. "Thank you for your time, and a very stimulating conversation."

"Detective Peabody will escort you out."

Alone, Eve sat, thought through that stimulating conversation.

She expected Bardov would at least put out feelers to try to find the nephew. He'd do that for form, or from habit. But she doubted he'd expend much time or energy. As he would have if she'd told him his nephew would have rolled on him for immunity.

And he'd told the truth about a woman with child being sacred.

He hadn't put those bullets in her victim, nor had anyone done so on his orders.

More, he hadn't known about the body behind the wall.

So until DeWinter came through, she had nothing.

16

As Eve started back to her office, Peabody hurried in her direction.

"Wow. I have to say wow! Maybe Bardov looks like your great-uncle, the friendly librarian, but you know he's a criminal overlord and you so totally handled him."

"Did I?"

"Oh yeah, you did. Wait. Wait." Catching the tone, Peabody snatched at Eve's arm. "You did. Sure, maybe he'll do a little poking around to satisfy himself, but he listened to you, Dallas. I watched him listening, taking it in. And maybe it's not the straight line, but you telling him Tovinski's going to live a long time not just caged up but living in fear? That hit the right mark with him. Because it's true, and he knows it. Just like he knows it's true you'd go after him if he takes Tovinski out.

"That's handling," Peabody insisted, "and that's keeping Tovinski alive, that's nailing down justice for Alva and Delgato. That's a fucking win."

"Well." The fire in Peabody's eyes burned away the weight on Eve's shoulders. "I'll return the wow."

"Fucking A!"

"Do me a solid and write it up. I want a copy in the case file I left on your desk and another for the unidentified remains. Then contact Bolton Singer and let him know his site's clear."

"Got it. He was telling the truth about the sanctity of pregnant women. Or he doesn't remember making an exception in this case."

"Oh, he'd remember. Whoever she was, however she ended up behind that wall, it wasn't on his orders."

When she stepped back into the bullpen, she caught Jenkinson's long stare. Despite the tie, she walked to his desk. "Do you figure I can't hold my own with an eightysomething-year-old gangster, Detective?"

"You hold your own, LT. Some of us are old enough to remember when Yuri Bardov wouldn't have shown his face in a cop shop unless he was in cuffs."

Jenkinson looked around the detectives' bullpen. "Well, one of us is old enough."

"Did you ever tangle with him?"

"Not directly. When I was still in uniform, back when you were still in diapers, I had a weasel. An asshole, liked to play big shot, but he had his ear to the street. So he tells me he's hearing about a big one coming up. Weapons deal. Now, back then, Bardov was all over the weapons trade, had a pipeline going up and down 95. Weasel says he's got a meet on it and he'll pass on what he gets, how it's going to cost me big. Next day, he's floating in the East River, throat slit with a dead rat tied around it.

"Guy was an asshole."

"But he was your asshole."

"Yeah. His hands look clean, Dallas. They ain't. Never have been."

"No question of that. What's his deal with women and kids?"

"Never touched the sex trade. Word was he felt it was beneath him. Gunrunning, cybercrime, booze, the protection racket, all that, but no sex trade and no kiddie porn or exploitation."

"Okay, so he's got a code, or a line he won't cross."

"You could say," Jenkinson agreed. "I remember—my gold shield's still shiny—there was a task force working on a child porno ring. Getting close, that was the buzz. Before they nailed it down, every one of the ringmasters ended up dead.

"Organized hits," Jenkinson said, "coordinated, professional hits. It had Bardov all over it, Loo. Couldn't pin it on him."

Now he shrugged. "Maybe they didn't try so hard."

Jenkinson gave her that long stare again. "You would've. You don't have to mourn the fucking perverts to do the job. Are you looking at him for something?"

"He doesn't fit. Pregnant woman, shot, maybe thirty-five to forty years ago, as yet unidentified. Walled up in the wine cellar of an old building—old restaurant."

"The other Hudson Yards case. Yeah, I heard some of it."

Absently, he fiddled with his tie. Eve's eyeballs vibrated.

"Not going to be Bardov. Not a pregnant woman. The bastard has a code, like you said. And he loves kids. Doesn't put a fucking halo on him, but he loves kids."

"He's got four." Eve reached back to the backgrounds she'd run. "Two of each, and no criminal on any of them—or their kids. No connections I found to his organization."

"Wouldn't be any. The story goes he fell for this Russian girl—like a friend of a cousin—and fell hard. He was already taking over—who the hell was it?—Smirnoff—like the vodka—Smirnoff's territory. Had a rep, wasn't afraid of doing his own wet work. This is before my time. I ain't that old."

She gazed up at the ceiling. "Add it all up, I'm betting we could get you twenty years. Twenty to twenty-five. With good behavior—which I don't think you can pull off—you could, maybe, get out in fifteen."

She smiled at him, fiercely. "Want to try it?"

"What do you want? And don't tell me this is about Alva. You didn't even know her. You looking for a score? Looking for something under the table?"

"A bribe? Are you offering me a payoff for tucking all this away?"

"I asked what you want."

"I'll tell you. Hold on a second." She took out her 'link. "Hey, Nadine. Locked and loaded?"

"You bet."

"Pull the trigger."

"Consider it done."

"Thanks." She put the 'link away. "I'll tell you what I want. What I want right down to my bones. I want you to spend the rest of your life in prison for what you did to Alva, for the shit you've smeared on your badge. That's what I want. Now, what I'll take?"

She folded her hands on the file. "You own up to what you've done, sign a statement thereof. You resign—immediately—and we'll deal it down to five years inside. If you can keep yourself in check, you'll probably get out in three, maybe three and a half. But you'll never carry a badge again."

"Fuck you."

"That's your answer? Let me tell you why you're going to take that back, and the time inside just went up to seven years. Right now, as we speak, Alva's story, those photos and documents, pages from her books, they're all over the media. Not just in New York, Wicker, all over. All the way out to Oklahoma. I expect your 'link's going to start blowing up really soon now."

"You're lying."

She just smiled again, made a gun out of her index finger and thumb. "Bang. Trigger pulled. How fast do you figure the cops who've worked under you will take to turn on you? The mayor of your little cop kingdom, the council members who are going to have the media beating down their doors?"

His 'link signaled.

"You wanna take that? I can wait."

He yanked out his 'link, set his teeth when he read the display. He turned it off. "I can beat this. Then I'll sue you for the skin off your ass."

"Documentation, photographs, scientific data, and witnesses. Do you think nobody knew what you did to her? Do you think nobody ever noticed the black eyes, the splinted fingers? The county sheriff has men out right now, interviewing neighbors."

His face flushed with rage. "I'm not doing seven years."

Eve leaned forward. "Wanna bet?"

He punched out, but she was ready for it. She wanted to punch back, more than she could say, but she just shoved his bunched fist back. "Make that ten years."

Reo opened the door.

"Cher Reo, assistant prosecuting attorney for New York, entering Interview."

"And by 'link conference," Reo said as she sat and set up a tablet, "Marvin Williams, prosecuting attorney for Beaver County, Oklahoma. Mr. Williams and I have observed this interview, have read over the file. At this time, Mr. Wicker, we are prepared to offer you a plea bargain. A full confession, your permanent resignation from your current position as chief of police, and your sworn agreement to never pursue or hold another position in law enforcement. Which includes prison guard, security guard, hell, crossing guard positions, or any position of authority."

"Go to hell."

"Jesus Christ, Garrett." On-screen, the Oklahoma prosecutor dragged at his hair.

"And you go with her, you simpering fuck."

"Ten years," Reo said flatly. "Or we go to court, drag it all out—adding your second wife, from whom I have a statement—the attempt to assault an officer, every Tom, Dick, and Mary we find that you used excessive and/or unnecessary force on, and every other thing we can and will dig up. I'm betting it's a lot. I'm betting it's going to add up to fifty before we're done with you."

"Take the deal, Garrett. Take the ten, because I'm telling you as someone who's known you—or thought he did—for eight years, you'll do twice that or more if this goes to trial."

"She's fucking dead!" He shouted it, pounding the table. "Why do you give a shit about any of this? She's dead."

Eve pulled out her badge, slapped it on the table. "That's why. Because it's meant to protect and serve, not hurt and terrorize. Because she mattered."

She rose. "Take the deal or don't. I don't care about that, because you're done. You're finished." She picked up her badge. "And when you're inside a cage where you belong, and they will put you there, I'll still have this. Because it's got to matter. Because of people like you. Dallas, exiting Interview."

She stepped out, took a couple of breaths.

Garrett Wicker wasn't her father, she reminded herself. But he and Richard Troy ran the same vicious, violent road.

And she'd beaten them both.

"Okay then." She breathed out again. "Now it's done."

She saw Peabody come out of Observation, and recognized the cautious concern on her partner's face.

To eliminate it, she held out a fist for a bump. "Good job as the whiny, stick-up-the-ass subordinate."

"I thought so. You're not staying in for the finale?"

"He's finished. Sometimes you have to leave it to the lawyers. He'll take the ten, figuring he'll get out in maybe six. He figures he can do six."

Eve shook her head as they walked back. "But he won't get through the first year without screwing it up, going at one of the guards, getting into it with another inmate. He'll do the full dime, and maybe more."

"He never saw it coming."

"He wouldn't. He's not wired to believe he'd pay any price—especially because of a woman."

"Not just that, Dallas. You had it ultrafine. The timing, the media storm, the whole ball of 'tude. I thought you were going to punch him when he took that swing at you. But really, you did. Complete beatdown."

"We did." She pointed to her office so Peabody went with her. "Now it's done, so we move on."

"No hits on the missing persons search, citywide, statewide, nationally," Peabody told her. "I started a global, but—"

"She went missing in New York, so there should be something. Still, it's possible nobody but her killer knew she was here. Thin, but possible. Or any record's been lost in the fog of time.

"Coffee," she said, then walked over to look out her window.

"We can start a facial recognition for her ID," Eve began. "The likeness isn't complete, but we start it, it starts eliminating."

She took the coffee Peabody held out.

"A young Middle Eastern woman, maybe Muslim—and during a period when there were still some loud echoes of bigotry—in New York. A woman college age or just beyond . . . Grad school? She's got means—jewelry, shoes—superior health and all that, so higher education feels probable. Did she go to college in New York? It's an angle. Pregnant, and the remains indicate good prenatal care, so a doctor, an experienced midwife."

"The wedding ring," Peabody put in. "So most likely married."

"Most likely, but a young, attractive, pregnant woman might put on a ring to avoid questions or issues. If she had a purse—and her type would—it didn't fall in with her. Or the killer got it out when they built the wall.

"The wall, the brick, the timing, that's why we're going to Hudson Valley."

"Hot damn!"

"Start the facial recognition. We'll update when we have the completed sketch. I'll contact Roarke for the copter."

"Double hot damn!" Peabody executed a butt and shoulder wiggle. "Like mega burning damn."

"We just closed a two-pronged case. I don't want to hate you right now."

"When I contacted the Singer estate earlier, they said the Singers would meet with us. Briefly."

"Tag them back. Tell her we're coming. Make it all routine."

"Isn't it?"

"We won't know until we get there. When we're done there, we'll drop in on Bardov."

Peabody's eyes went to big brown moons. "Really?"

"Routine follow-up. I want to see if his memory matches theirs. Get going. I'll write up Wicker."

"I can take care of it."

"I want this one."

Understanding, Peabody just nodded. As she started out, she gave a butt wiggle. "Jet-copter ride!"

Eve weighed two choices whenever she faced air travel. She could pretend she remained on the ground by concentrating on something else—anything else—for the duration. This required never looking

out a window of any kind, and convincing herself any and all turbu-
lence was just the rumbling of traffic over a pothole.

In the street.

On the ground.

Because the size and amount of glass in a two-passenger jet-copter
took this option off the table, she had to count on Plan B and focus
every cell in her body on keeping what she considered a flying insect
aloft.

She didn't like the constant, low-level buzz reminding her she rode
in the belly of the insect. And insects often ended their short, an-
noying lives being swallowed up by a larger flying thing, or getting
swatted flat.

As Peabody loved every minute of buzzing around in the air like a
mosquito, when flying with her partner, Eve had to merge both options.

Eve hunched over her PPC, studiously reviewing data she'd already
committed to memory. Peabody plastered her face to the porthole in
the door Eve imagined could burst open any second and suck them out
so they pinwheeled screaming over the scenery Peabody rhapsodized
over.

"Oh, it's so pretty! The hills! The trees! I bet it's super-ult-mag in
the fall. All kinds of vineyards and orchards!"

"Go sit up with the pilot."

"Is it okay? I can see through here, but—"

"Go."

Peabody hopped up and all but danced the short distance to do her
rhapsodizing in front of the wide windscreen until they dropped, mer-
cifully, on the helipad.

The minute Eve got behind the wheel of the waiting car, everything
inside her settled. She put the return trip firmly out of her mind and
programmed the Singer estate.

"That was so quick." Still flushed with pleasure, Peabody strapped into the passenger seat. "McNab and I talked about taking a day trip up here, but decided we'd spend too much of the day getting here and back."

Eve gave her the next ninety seconds to chatter—"The hills! The green! The river!"

"Since we're not here to cozy up together in some quaint bed-and-breakfast, maybe you could focus on the people we're about to interview."

"I bet they have mag-o B and B's up here. Anyway, J. Bolton and Marvinia Singer are in residence, as is Elinor Singer. That's how they put it anyway. 'In residence.' So we can talk to all three of them in one place."

"Bardov's only a few miles from their estate, so we'll see if he's 'in residence' when we're done at the Singers'. I want to get a better sense of that relationship. It goes back decades."

"I can see why they all built up here. It's peaceful, and you can really spread out. And the scenery's the total. But it feels like, especially in Elinor Singer's time at the helm, she had to spend more time in the city than here."

"And it had to cost to maintain a country estate," Eve added. "Tough going in the couple years before the Urbans, a lot tougher going during."

"So you hook up—on a business level—with the deep pockets of a mob boss."

"A calculated business decision," Eve concluded. "But here you are, decades later and still hooked. And did that initial hook have anything to do with killing a pregnant woman and walling her up?"

"I gotta say, Dallas, it feels like Bardov would've been too smart for that. You don't hide the body, you get rid of it."

"Agreed. And I don't see him condoning that kind of hit. But it's time for these people to reach back in their memory banks."

She drove along a wall of white brick to an arching white gate. And rolled down her window to speak into the security intercom.

Good morning. Rosehill is a private estate. If you have an appointment, please state your name.

"Lieutenant Dallas and Detective Peabody." Eve held up her badge for the scan. "We're expected."

Welcome to Rosehill. Please proceed through the gate and continue directly to the main house. You will be met. Enjoy your visit.

The gates swung soundlessly open.

The drive ran arrow straight to the house. They'd gone with white brick there, too, in a three-story structure that struck Eve as more big and sturdy than elegant.

Generous windows, yes, and plenty of plantings to soften those straight lines, but no balconies or terraces, no gracious front porch or veranda.

"It's impressive," Peabody commented. "But it's not, you know, welcoming. It looks really stern and strict. Our house isn't going to look stern and strict."

"No chance of that."

"The front garden's nice, but there's just the long, long lawn up to it. No trees or anything. You've got some over there, way to the side, and they probably have a garden in the back, but otherwise, there's like this big blank green slate."

She shot Eve a look. "I'm paying a lot of attention because I've got landscaping on the brain, but inside that, it kind of speaks to who lives here."

"Agreed. It looks more like an institution than a home."

"That's it! And you get the feeling that everything inside runs on schedule. Or else."

Eve pulled up at the end of the drive. Since she didn't spot any other vehicles or a specified parking area, she left the car where it was.

The door, six feet across and twice that high in steel gray, opened as she and Peabody got out.

A man of about fifty, wearing Summerset black stood militarily straight. "Lieutenant, Detective. I'll show you where you may wait."

When she crossed the threshold, Eve's sense of an institution didn't fade. A well-endowed one, she thought as she scanned the grand foyer. A lot of dark, heavy furnishings, a lot of paintings of dour-looking people scowling out of dark, heavy frames.

A thick rug in red and gold tones spread over the floor to the straight-as-a-ruler staircase.

The man in black led them to a room off the right, where the generous window looked out over the foundation plantings and endless sea of green to the wall of white.

"May I take your coats?"

"No, we're good." Because it's cold in here, she thought. Not temperature-wise, but in every other sense.

"Please make yourselves comfortable. The Singers will join you shortly, and you'll have a tea and coffee service."

More dark, heavy furniture, more—to her eye—depressing art. More white brick in a fireplace framed by dark wood. The white walls were done in stripes—one matte, one gloss, one matte, and so on—in a style she found disorienting.

"Antiques," Peabody said, studying a deeply carved table. "Really valuable antiques, but too heavy for the room, you know? And you just want to strip off the decades of lacquer to get to the gorgeous wood under it."

"Why are you whispering?"

"It just sort of feels like you're expected to."

"Got your dust catchers here and there, but no family photos. Not a single one. And what's growing all over that couch?"

"Cabbage roses. It's really old-fashioned and, again, just too much. And the millwork's gorgeous, but with the white-on-white walls, it's all wrong. I mean the walls are wrong. I'm taking mental pictures so I know what not to do."

Eve heard the approaching footsteps—quick, female—and turned to the doorway.

Her first thought—though she'd studied Marvinia Singer's ID shot—was the woman looked completely out of place in the cold, institutional air of the house.

Her hair swung in rich brown, chin-length curves around a pretty face warmed with a smile. She wore a bright blue shirt with a long tail over simple black leggings. Blue-and-silver twists dangled from her ears with a small diamond stud winking from the left cartilage.

Her voice rang like a bell. "Oh, I'm so sorry we've kept you waiting. I'm Marvinia Singer." She stuck out a hand, gripped, and gave Eve's a hearty shake before doing the same with Peabody's. "My husband and his mother will be right along. Please, please, sit down. I'm delighted to meet you. How is Roarke, Lieutenant? I haven't run into him in months."

"He's fine, thank you."

"I'm sure he is. I'm hearing really wonderful things about An Didean. Such a brilliant and generous undertaking. I'm hoping to arrange a tour of it very soon."

She gestured to two chairs of the same rusty red as the enormous couch roses, then settled in the corner of the couch.

"My son tells me you found the person who killed that poor woman. I know it's a relief to him, to all of us, to know that man's been caught."

"Yuri Bardov's nephew."

The smile left her eyes. "Yes, so I heard. I'm sorry to hear it. I'm very fond of Marta."

"You're friendly with Mrs. Bardova?"

"Yes. She's been very generous to my foundation. And we're neighbors, women with some common interests. I haven't spoken with her since I heard. It feels wrong, even for a friend, to speak to her of this right now. I know she and Yuri treated Alexei as one of their own."

"You know him?"

"Not well, no. His wife, Nadia, has again given some time to my foundation and I'm grateful. I can't conceive she knew he was capable of doing what he did. I can't believe Marta had any idea he was stealing from her husband, from us. Am I correct you're here to ask us about all of that?"

"In part, yes."

"It may seem biased for me to say, as a woman, a mother, that neither of these women, these mothers, were aware. But I believe it, absolutely. I've known Marta for—God—nearly fifty years."

"And Yuri?"

"He's less . . . knowable. I have talked to him more in the last few years than previously, as he's actually a very skilled gardener, and I've asked his advice in that area."

She glanced toward the doorway before she continued, "I'm not unaware of Yuri's reputation, but can tell you I haven't seen that side of him, if true, in the years I've known Marta. Alexei . . . the phrase is *a lean and hungry look*. I would have applied that to him."

"He and your son are about the same age," Peabody said.

"Yes. Different interests, different circles. And Bolt was a few years older when Alexei came to the country, and already had his established friends, and then was off to college. They never clicked."

Eve heard more footsteps and noted Marvinia's glance at the doorway. "And here we are."

Eve turned her head to watch the entrance.

J. Bolton, trim, tanned, tall in his pearl-gray linen suit, his hair a shining wave of golden blond, had his mother's hand tucked in his crooked arm.

His smile was all charm and dancing eyes.

Elinor Singer wore a white long-sleeved dress all but cracking with starch. Her hair, gold like her son's, slicked back from her face to form a hard knot at the base of her neck.

She'd gone with a suite of rubies: bloodred orbs at her ears, another at her throat, a circle of them on one wrist, another on her finger.

On her left hand the bright white diamond cut the air like a knife.

Her eyes glinted, hard blue. Eve wondered how many treatments it took to get every line and wrinkle stretched and erased out of century-old skin.

"What a treat!" Singer patted his mother's hand as they walked. "The famous Dallas and Peabody in our parlor. I'm J. B. Singer. Lieutenant Dallas, Detective Peabody, let me introduce you to my mother, Elinor Bolton Singer."

Elinor took the corner of the couch opposite her daughter-in-law. Singer sat between them.

"Isn't this lovely?" Singer began.

"Don't be a dolt," Elinor snapped, and, like her skin, her voice was drum-tight. "They want us to gossip about the Bardovs. You're wasting everyone's time. We don't gossip in this house."

Strict and stern, Eve thought, came from the top.

"No point in wasting time," Eve said in return. "So how about we talk about murder?"

19

Elinor's expression didn't change—then again, Eve wasn't sure it could.

"As you've arrested Alexei Tovinski and the thief Carmine Delgato is dead, we have nothing more to say on the subject. The woman was trespassing, but her transgression exposed crimes against our company. We will, of course, take steps to ensure such difficulties don't happen again."

"Will you continue your association with Bardov Construction?" Eve asked.

She lifted an eyebrow a fraction of an inch. "That association is legal. The Bardov organization, like ours, was victimized. I would assume they, as we, will take all necessary steps to prevent any future thievery or exploitation. If you've come here to intimate that the Singer organization or any member of my family played a part in this thievery, exploitation, or the death of a trespasser, I would suggest you leave now. You may address your remarks to our attorneys."

"Now, Mother." Singer reached for Elinor's hand. She swatted his away.

"Our victimization continues with honking media gossip and innuendo. I will not have it. An employee, one who should not have been trusted, stole from and conspired to steal from us. From the very people who provided him with employment, with the wherewithal to make a good living. And we're to be questioned?"

"This is a very upsetting time for you," Peabody began.

"You know nothing of it. Our reputation has been smeared by this. Our efforts to create a space of beauty and function will be forever besmirched by this woman's death."

"Her name was Alva Quirk," Eve said, voice cold. "And I'd say her family's finding this a pretty difficult time."

"Perhaps if her family had done more to preserve family, she wouldn't have lived on the streets, nor ended up dead in a dumpster."

"Elinor, please!"

Elinor spared her daughter-in-law a glance. "You will make heroes of them. Your downtrodden and underserved. I have nothing more to say on the subject. So if that's all—"

"It's not," Eve said as Elinor started to rise.

The butler and two women—also in black—filed in carrying trays. A coffee service, a tea service, china.

Without a word, they arranged it all on the table between the sofa and chairs. One of the women poured tea into a cup, passed it to Elinor.

"I'll do the rest, thank you." Marvinia rose. "Coffee, tea?"

"Coffee, black," Eve said. "My partner takes cream and sugar. The Alva Quirk case is closed. Of course, if more information comes to light, we'll reopen it. We're here about another murder."

She took the coffee from Marvinia, but she watched Elinor.

"A woman, early twenties, in the last trimester of pregnancy, murdered on another Singer construction site."

"Nonsense," Elinor decreed. "What site? We've heard nothing of this, and surely would have."

"You no longer own the site. Roarke Industries does."

Elinor managed a smirk. "Then I would suggest you look to your own."

"That would be a waste of time."

"I'd expect you to say so. But one does hear what one does hear about Roarke."

Eve just sipped some coffee. "Since gossip isn't allowed here, we'll skip over that."

She heard Marvinia choke back a laugh.

"But it would be a waste of time because the murder occurred thirty-seven years ago. And Singer was the owner and developer of record."

"I did hear something about this." Marvinia spoke again. "Something about human remains found on another development project in Hudson Yards. A woman, you said. And pregnant?"

"That's right. We're in the process of identifying her."

Eve took out her PPC, brought up the sketch. Held it up.

"Oh, poor thing. So young!"

"Does she look familiar?"

"I can't say I recognize her," Singer said. "Thirty-seven years. A very long time."

"She could be anyone." Elinor dismissed it. "Likely a squatter, one who came to a bad end."

"We recovered certain items that indicate she wasn't squatting. My questions, at this point, center on the time frame, her identity, and how her body was concealed."

"Concealed?" Marvinia shook her head. "I assumed she'd been buried."

"Not exactly, no. Mr. Singer, you were running the company at that time. Though, of course, Mrs. Singer, you were still very much involved. Do either of you recall an employee or subcontractor going missing?"

"No," Singer said immediately.

"It was difficult to keep good employees during that time," Elinor added. "To find and keep the skilled and responsible. Many were transients, or simply unskilled and looking for any kind of work. Most of those didn't last. We could hardly, considering the circumstances, remember who came and went."

"It seems a young woman about thirty-two weeks pregnant would be more memorable than most. She was Middle Eastern, in excellent health."

Singer stared. "How could you know all that? You said you hadn't identified her."

"Our forensic anthropologist has examined the remains. As has the chief medical examiner. This woman was shot, three times, with a thirty-two-caliber weapon."

"Oh my God." Marvinia pressed a hand to her mouth as her eyes glistened. "The baby. How horrible."

"Part of your project on this site was a restaurant. The plans included a wine cellar, which required some excavation. We've established at the time of the murder, the foundation and the exterior cellar walls were in place. We haven't located records of the specific work or the building inspections."

Elinor let out a dismissive huff. "Study your history, girl. There was still considerable turmoil, and the building trade was rife with corruption. Those of us trying to rebuild the city the mobs had done their best to destroy did what we could and how we could. Most building inspectors expected cash payment if they troubled themselves to come to a site. It took months, years, for the system to right itself."

"But you remember this project? Bardov was, again, a financial partner."

"If you believe Yuri Bardov had some pregnant girl killed, speak to him."

"I have, and I will again. Now I'm speaking to you. You remember this project, Mr. Singer?"

"I do, of course. We were more focused, and further along with the River Park project, the signature tower—which we're proud still stands. The site you're speaking of was more of a mix of quickly constructed affordable housing and commercial spaces. All making use—on both sites—of what we'd begun before the Urbans.

"But, as Mother said, post-war was a complicated, chaotic time." With a sorrowful smile, Singer spread his hands. "In the end, the South-West project simply wasn't profitable enough to continue. We sold off a considerable portion of it and, again, focused on River Park and other projects."

"But before you sold a portion of the property, this restaurant—which opened spring of 2025 as the Skyline—and several other buildings were completed."

"Oh yes. Several of the commercial spaces were occupied, if memory serves, and several of the low-rise residential buildings as well when we sold."

"Who was in charge of the restaurant's construction? The job boss, the foreman? The mason and so on?"

"Oh my goodness." With a half laugh, he sat back. "Nearly forty years? Longer than either of you have been alive and nearly half my own life? My memory isn't nearly that good."

Eve turned to Elinor. "How's yours?"

"As I said, it was difficult to find and keep skilled labor at that time. J.B. and I struggled over that very issue. But I do recall we decided to promote Joe Kendall—a longtime employee—to foreman on several buildings on that site. You remember Joe Kendall, J.B.?"

"A blast from the past," he said with a laugh. "Yes, I remember

Joe. Big as a house, smoked like a chimney. He may have handled the restaurant—the one with the wine cellar. We had several buildings earmarked for restaurant use, I think. I know Joe took on a few of the commercial buildings.

"God, I haven't thought of Big Joe in years."

"He no longer works for Singer?"

"He's been gone twenty years—or nearly. Smoked like a chimney, loved food—especially fried—and carried at least thirty extra pounds."

"I remember him," Marvinia murmured. "From the holiday parties. He had such a big laugh. He always called me Miss Marvinia. He had a wife and a couple of children. He wouldn't have hurt anyone, Lieutenant."

"That's not for us to say," Elinor corrected.

"There was a discrepancy in materials."

"Of what sort?" Elinor demanded.

"The exterior walls are concrete and block—substandard."

"Material was hard to come by, and there was considerable price gouging. The goal was quick, and with hopes updating would be done at some point. As it is being done now."

"An interior wall was constructed about three feet inside that exterior wall. Brick. Good-quality brick and mortar were used. The ceiling—or the floor of the main restaurant over just this area—was formed and poured using good-quality concrete."

"She was . . ." Marvinia rubbed a hand over her heart. "They walled her in? Her and the baby?"

"Yes. They had to access the brick—much higher quality than anything on that site at that time. Where would they access it, and so quickly? You had other projects."

Singer held up a finger. "I see! Someone who worked on, or perhaps even a supervisor on that site could have—would have—known where we had a supply of brick. Either warehouses, or on another site.

But, dear, if you're asking me to try to remember missing material from that time, a shortfall? I couldn't possibly."

"That's what they counted on." Marvinia turned to him. "Darling, that's what they counted on. Someone stole it, they'd say, or like with Alexei, they doctored an invoice, or amount. Oh, this is just so sad. Think of that girl's family. What they've gone through. Not knowing. All these years."

"Stop fancifying," Elinor ordered. "For all you know she had no family. Or they booted her when she got pregnant."

"If they did, shame on them," she bit back, and from the look in Elinor's eye, Marvinia didn't bite often. "And that doesn't change what happened. J.B., you have to think back, look back."

"Of course I will, my sweet. But honestly, nearly four decades. Sketchy records, lost records, workers coming and going. And I confess, my focus was much more on River Park at that time. The other?"

He looked at Eve, lifted his hands. "It was get it up as best we could. Businesses, ours included, were bleeding money. So we took partners, did what we could to increase revenue while trying to build. To give people some normality again. We did our best in a difficult time."

"I'm sure you did. But if you would think back and if you have any records from that time we've so far been unable to access, we need them.

"Peabody."

"Yes, sir. We have a warrant for records, invoices, inventory lists. I'll print that out for you now."

"A warrant." Singer held up his hands again. "Hardly necessary. We're more than willing to cooperate."

"Even so." Eve rose as Peabody used her PPC to print out the warrant. "We expect to have the victim's identity verified within the next forty-eight hours. Employee records are also included in the warrant. She was on your property when she was killed, so she may have had business there."

"Or she was trespassing."

Eve nodded at Elinor. "We'll find out. Trust me. This case is as important as Alva Quirk's. Thank you for your time, your cooperation, and the coffee."

"I'll show you out." Marvinia rose, walked them to the door. "I'm so sorry I can't be more help. I've never taken an interest in the business. But I'll do what I can to nudge J.B.'s memory."

"And your mother-in-law's?"

"Well, Elinor remembers what she chooses and how she chooses. But the company's reputation is everything to her. She'll do whatever she can to end this and move on from it."

"I'm sure she will. Thanks again."

As they walked to the car, Peabody glanced back at the house. "It must be hard."

Eve got behind the wheel, took one last look herself. "What's that?"

"I'm guessing in a house this size, they each have their own wing, but still, it must be hard to live in the same house as your mother-in-law when you really don't like her."

"And knowing the person you really don't like is top of the food chain." Eve did a three-point turn to head out. "They travel a lot, have a couple other homes in other places, but they use this as home base. Why do you figure?"

"Well, Elinor might have had her skin stretched so tight you could bounce a five-dollar credit off her cheek, but she's still over the century mark. That's one."

"That's one, but my take is it's mostly habit. J.B. was never really head of the company, and didn't want to be. All that shows in his background. She's ruled right along. And when he took on a project, he was mostly crap at it. She let him be. That's indulgence. He married money and status, so points in his favor. But Marvinia has her own life and interests."

"I looked into her foundation a little, and they do good work."

"Good work, and she's not just a figurehead. She's involved—and not involved in the Singer family business. Probably points for her on Elinor's scale. So they maintain a polite if cool relationship because they both indulge J.B."

Eve made a turn, following the computer's prompts for the Bardov estate. "Even though he's weak, spoiled, and a liar."

"I felt like he was lying, but I couldn't catch it."

"Taps his foot—right foot—when he's lying. Looks you straight in the eye, doesn't evade or hesitate, but that foot tapping? Major tell."

"I missed that! I hate when I miss stuff like that."

"His mother's a better liar. No tells there. Just icy contempt. Anyway, they knew the victim was down there, so they didn't sell off that section of the property. I'm wondering now if Bolton Singer sold it to Roarke before they could stop him."

"Or maybe they thought, after all this time, it wouldn't matter."

"Maybe. Whether they walled her up or not, that's for us to find out. But what I know is they walled her right out of their minds. She didn't matter. Forget her, move on."

"If they killed her or had her killed . . ."

"That's an if, but one way or the other, they knew. I don't care how much chaos or corruption was going on, Elinor Bolton Singer damn well knew if a freaking truckload of bricks went missing. And she knew a wall of high-quality bricks went up in a cheap build. I'm saying she knew why. She knew."

Peabody shifted as Eve pulled up to another gate, gleaming black in the opening of the stone walls.

"Young, pregnant woman—pretty woman. J.B. has a little roll

there, and oops. She decides to have the baby. Maybe he tries to pay her off, but as it gets closer to the time, she wants more. More support, acknowledgment. Maybe she loved him, or he promised the usual. Leave my wife, and all that bullshit."

As her thoughts had run the same, Eve nodded. "Makes her a threat. He lures her up there. Maybe he planned to scare her, or threaten her back, or offer her more money. Whatever, it didn't end well. He panics, or loses his temper, or he planned to get rid of her all along."

"He gets the brick. It would be easy for him. I guess he could build a wall. I mean he grew up around construction."

"Sloppy build. Solid enough, but sloppy. Yeah, he could've done it. Then he tells Mother all—or he tells her before and she tells him how to handle it. That works for me because they knew. They knew her face when they saw the sketch. They knew she was down there."

She rolled down the window.

"Lieutenant Dallas, Detective Peabody to see Mr. Bardov."

Instead of a computer-generated response, Eve watched a man— big and burly—walk to the gate.

She got out of the car, approached from her side.

"You're not expected."

"No." But she expected he had a weapon under his suit coat. "We conducted an interview in the area and hoped Mr. Bardov would be available to speak with us. A follow-up to our conversation yesterday."

"Wait."

When he walked away, Eve took the time to study the view through the gate.

Trees, green and leafy with early summer. A winding drive, a green lawn with groupings of flowering shrubs, some sort of stone structure where water tumbled.

All dominated by the big house of dusky blue with its generous terraces, glass rails, tall windows, and wide, covered porch where flowering vines wound up thick columns.

No strict and stern here, she thought. Inhabited by a mobster, yes, guarded by armed security, no doubt, but with a facade, at least, of welcome.

The guard came back. "Mr. Bardov is pleased to meet with you and offer you refreshments in the garden. You may go to the house, and Mrs. Bardova will show you the way."

"Thanks."

She got back in the car.

"It's beautiful," Peabody said. "And I know it's probably built on the crushed bones of his enemies, but it still looks sort of like a mansion in a fairy tale.

"That water feature. I wonder if I can build something like that."

Eve nearly stopped the car. "Build?"

"It would be a fun project—maybe next spring. I've never built anything like that." Peabody craned her neck as Eve drove past it. "I think I could."

"You baffle me, Peabody. Sometimes you just baffle the crap right out of me."

Before they reached the house, a woman came out on the porch.

Like Marvinia, Marta Bardova wore simple leggings and an overshirt, hers in bright red with some frills down the front. Tendrils of silvery-blond hair escaped from the loosely bundled knot on top of her head.

"Welcome to our home," she said when Eve got out of the car. "I'm Marta Bardova. I'm starstruck." She laughed as she pressed a hand to her heart. "I so loved *The Icove Agenda*, even though I wept for the babies. Oh, those babies broke my heart."

She held out her hand to shake. A ringless hand, Eve noted, of a woman who smelled like . . . sugar cookies.

"Detective Peabody." Marta shook again. "I have to ask you a personal question."

"Um. Okay."

"McNab. In the book, and now in the new book, he's your love. Is he?"

"Ah, yes. We're . . ."

"I'm so glad!" Beaming, Marta clapped her hands together. "He's adorable. In the books, he's adorable. I wish you many happy years together. Please, come in. Yuri's working in the garden. My granddaughter brought her twins to visit."

"We're sorry to interrupt," Eve began.

"No, no. We're baking, so you'll have lemonade and cookies. They'll be thrilled."

Here was color, Eve thought as Marta led them through the house. Lofty ceilings, open space, happy colors, and floods of light, vases everywhere filled with flowers.

And the smell of sugar cookies.

"You've beaten the storms they say are coming," Marta continued. "It should be nice to have a talk in the garden while the sun shines."

Eve heard squealing, a female voice order someone named *Nicholas Michael Cobain!* to *Stop that right now*, followed by laughter.

Marta rolled her eyes. "Our great-grandson is a handful."

Eve spotted the handful—around four, she guessed, all curly headed and caramel skinned and wickedly gleaming eyes—squeezing some pink stuff out of a tube onto a girl—obviously his twin.

"I make a flower on Tasha, Mama!"

The girl, a near mirror image of her brother, squeezed something green out of a tube. It shot out in a stream, hit him right below the left eye.

Hilarity ensued.

"My charming and perfectly behaved family."

The woman currently refereeing looked over, sighed. "We're a mess, Mama. So sorry."

"Messes clean up. But how will the cookies get decorated if you decorate each other?"

The girl offered an angelic smile. "We taste good!"

"Let me see." Marta walked to the wide kitchen island, bent down, made smacking noises on the girl's arm, the boy's face. "Good enough to eat. Now pretend you're good children and say hello to our guests."

"Hello!" they chorused.

"Well done. Just this way," she added, and gestured to the wide opening where the glass doors had been folded back to let in the June day.

Peabody actually gasped, and had Marta pausing to look at her.

"It's—it's just glorious. Your gardens. And another water feature, the arbors! Oh, and the play area for the kids. The flagstone paths, with moss. It's the good witch's garden. I have to steal these ideas. We're going to start gardens and landscaping."

"You garden?"

"When I can. But not like this. I haven't worked in a garden like this since I came to New York. Smell the peonies! I'm sorry." She caught herself—or Eve's bland stare caught her.

"Yuri will be delighted. And you must talk to him about your gardening. I dig and plant where he tells me, but this is his."

She led them down one of the paths, beyond a knoll buried in flowers, through a screen of slim trees to where the mob boss, in dirt-stained baggies, a faded blue shirt, and a straw hat, sat on a low, rolling stool, doing something to what even Eve recognized as a tomato plant.

"Yuri, your guests."

"Yes, welcome, yes. One second."

"Epsom salt mixture," Peabody said. "For the magnesium."

He looked over in approval. "You know."

"Your gardens are amazing, Mr. Bardov."

"They're work, and the work is my pleasure." He rose, dusted his gloved hands on his pants.

"You'll talk," Marta said. "And when you're ready, there will be lemonade and strangely decorated cookies on the patio."

"Thank you, *lyubimaya*."

Eve recognized the look in his eye as he watched his wife walk away. And wondered if she'd still see the same in Roarke's for her when they were eighty.

"So," he said. "There's more for us to discuss?"

"We came to the area to speak with Elinor, J. Bolton, and Marvinia Singer. And thought we'd conduct a follow-up with you, as we're here."

"Ah, Marvinia. A lovely woman. She and my Marta are good friends."

"So she told us."

"I fear Elinor will be displeased with me, for Alexei's sins. What can you do? So, Alexei, he's on his way to his new life?"

"I'm sure you know he is."

Bardov smiled. "You and your associates have done an excellent job. I don't believe I'll waste time, any more time, on Alexei. He's hurt and disappointed his aunt and, for me, this is a bigger sin than the theft. She shed tears for him, but they're done now. Our granddaughter brought the twins to make her happy. They do."

"They were decorating each other more than the cookies," Peabody told him, and now he flashed a grin.

"Children are the light that cuts through any shadow. You don't ask, but I'll tell you. We've gone to see and reassure Nadia. She's family, her children are our children. As are the others. They'll be cherished and tended as children should be.

"Now." He gestured and began to walk. "Tell me why you came. You don't worry I'll hunt for Alexei. The woman he killed, I know, is to be laid to rest by her family, in her home. As I know the man who once beat her, treated her cruelly will now be punished for it."

"You know quite a lot."

He nodded at Eve, stopped to pull small snippers from his baggies. He cut a fat red peony and offered it to Peabody. "You enjoy the scent."

"Yes. Thank you."

"I know quite a lot because I have an interest. You and Detective Peabody are of interest to me. At one time of my life, this interest would have had a different purpose. But these days, I enjoy my gardens, I think to get chickens. The children would enjoy them. I think a puppy. It's time, as old Boris died in his sleep last winter. I think I have years ahead and will spend them with the gardens and the children, the chickens, the dog. Two dogs," he said with a nod. "We'll get two puppies."

The idea seemed to please him as he took off his gardening gloves.

"The . . . pursuit?" he continued. "The interest in such things wanes. I wonder if your husband would like to buy my company."

"I'm sorry, what?"

"I have no one to leave it to now. It would have been Alexei's. How foolish he was to steal what would have been his own in only a few years. My children have other lives, and are not involved in this part of mine. I'm grateful for that now. I see Marta was wise to insist. So, I think I am retired."

He nodded again. "I'll be speaking to Roarke. But that's another world from this, from you coming to see me. This is about the woman, the one with child. I have thought of her since I learned. I've asked some questions, but I don't have any answers for you."

"Would you tell me if you did?"

"Yesterday, ah, perhaps, perhaps not. Today, I'm retired." He smiled, radiating charm. "Yes, I would. I would accept your way of justice today. And I hope, tomorrow. She haunts me. I have no face to give her, but she haunts me. I ate in the restaurant with my family, many times, with her and the child trapped under our feet. I would help you if I could."

Eve pulled out her PPC. "Let me give you her face."

20

BARDOV STUDIED THE SKETCH, THEN CROOKED HIS FINGER.

He sat on a bench and, when Eve sat beside him, studied the sketch again.

"A man in the line of work from which I have retired must remember faces. I remember faces. I don't know hers. Didn't know hers," he corrected. "I'm sorry I can't tell you who she was. But I know I'll remember her face now.

"Will you find her?"

"I will. We will."

"Good." He put his hands on his thighs. "She had a mother, perhaps my age now. Her mother should know."

"How closely was your business aligned with the Singers when the woman in this sketch died?"

"They had more trouble than me. I had ways to profit from the . . . unrest. Some still call it unrest. Ways I won't detail to cops on such a pretty day. We can say my interests were more diverse, and not so bound up in building and development. So during the time this young woman died, and the push for building ran hot, the Singers, and others, required backing. Loans or influence."

"Such as knowing which inspectors to bribe, what official to blackmail?"

"Such as," he said with a smile. "Though Elinor still pulled most strings, J.B. was the titular head and he would have his vanity project."

"The Singer Tower."

"Yes. It had survived the unrest, but hadn't been completed and, as many buildings did, had damage—from the unrest, from squatters. He had a vision, and not a bad one for all that. For the tower, for the lesser buildings to accent it. He poured the company into that, and gave less to the—ah, what did they call it?"

"South-West, or Hudson Yards Skyline, depending on the records."

"Yes, yes, I remember. I like better Roarke's Hudson Yards Village. Be that as it may, J.B. overweighted his outlay—he's a poor businessman— and they needed backing. I—my company—made them a loan, taking a ten percent interest. On both sites. Elinor was not pleased."

At his satisfied smile, Eve spoke her mind. "You don't like her."

"She's a dislikable woman, as I'm sure you found her. But business is business, and it wasn't my problem, was it, if J.B. accepted the terms so quickly, and without fully informing her. So we became partners of a sort, and that's continued on a few projects over the years. Such as the River View project—the renewal of it—where Alexei killed the woman."

He sat back. "You wonder if they knew of my other . . . my diversity at the time we made this partnership. Of course, but business is business. You wonder if they ever came to me for a favor. This might be true. It might be true I granted that favor and took one in return. Business."

He gestured toward an emerald-green bird that hovered with a blur of wings at a red flower.

"Hummingbirds are so industrious. And such a bright sight in any garden. They're very territorial, and will fight off their own kids to drink their fill."

He smiled again.

"You wonder if favors continue. If the grandson now in the big office asks for favors from me or seeks my influence. And I can say he doesn't. I can say he's not the businessperson his grandmother was, but a far better one than his father. This is a low bar," Bardov added with a laugh.

He looked at Eve. "This is why you're here. For the gossip."

"Yeah, you could say."

"I like gossip. It adds some spice to the bland."

"Did J.B. have affairs? Were there other women?"

Bardov's eyebrows winged up. "Juice as well as spice. Some men can love with their heart, but their body wants more, and their mind allows this by believing it doesn't matter. Or count. Or hurts no one. The mind lies. But what J.B.'s faithfulness matters in this . . . Oh, oh, I see."

He went silent a moment, brows drawn together now.

"You wonder if J.B. indulged himself with this young woman. A much younger woman than his wife, as many men look for. We're not friends, you see. I'm not a confidant or someone he'd speak to about his infidelity."

"But you know he had affairs."

"It pays to know a partner's weaknesses. I know that for a time and, during this time, there was dispute, tension. As I said, Marta and Marvinia are friends. They are confidantes."

"Tensions because he cheated?"

"No, not that precisely. Tensions that may have allowed his mind to justify breaking his vows. Their son didn't want the business. He wanted music, the freedom of it. The fame from it. He has talent, and his mother very much wanted him to pursue his dreams. I know she and Elinor fought over that and Marvinia, outnumbered as J.B. won't

music at the conservatory. Classical music. I wasn't much on classics, but when she played, you were transported. I think I fell in love with her when she played."

His hand trembled a little when he picked up the sketch again.

"I was her first. She'd never been with anyone, so we took that part slow. Well, slow for me at nineteen. And we just . . . fell. Crazy about each other, wrapped up in ourselves and our music."

Carefully, in a room crowded with regrets and grief, he laid the sketch down again. "After about a year, we moved off campus, got a little apartment together. If her parents had known, they'd have yanked her back, or tried. She'd say she couldn't tell them. And I'd say, you're an adult. You can make your own decisions."

He sat back, eyes closed again. "Arrogant, so arrogant. I didn't understand how hard it was for her to stand up to her family when I was so busy pushing away from my own. But we were happy, we made it work. We were so young, and we were careless. She got pregnant."

He straightened, reached for his wife's hand as she perched on the arm of his chair.

"I was terrified and saw my life going up in smoke. We talked about choices, but in her heart, from her upbringing and beliefs, she didn't have a choice. So, we're going to have a baby."

He pressed his wife's hand to his cheek.

"What did your family say?" Eve asked him.

"Nothing. They didn't know. I never told them about Johara. My business and fuck them."

"Bolt."

"That's how I felt about everything back then. They wanted me back in New York, working sites or a desk. Carrying on the Singer legacy."

He dragged his hands through his hair. "I wanted none of that. I wanted music, the stage. And Johara.

"We were going to get married. She said she needed to go back to London first. She needed to talk to her parents. She needed their blessing. I needed their blessing, after she'd spoken to them. I can tell you I didn't want that. I fought that. We fought."

He blew out a breath. "We made up long enough to exchange vows—not legal, which I didn't want anyway. Who needs a contract? That's all bullshit."

He breathed out, then scrubbed his hands over his face. "Young and stupid, and selfish. I was so goddamn selfish. But we had a little ceremony, just the two of us. I didn't realize she'd done that to soften leaving. She left me a note and said she had to do the right thing for her family, for the baby, for our future."

"When was that?"

"Ah . . ." He set the brandy aside, pressed his fingers to his eyes. "In April. April of 2024. She was, um, about four months along. Just starting to show. And I don't know, maybe she panicked a little. We weren't going to be able to keep it just our thing much longer."

"What did you do?"

"I was so mad. I tried calling her, but she didn't answer. I thought about going after her, but, Christ, I didn't have the money. And I didn't know where her parents lived. I waited. I worked, took gigs, wrote really bad songs. I didn't hear from her until June, more than a month. I was out of my mind, pissed off with it, and I get a letter. An actual letter."

He took another moment, leaning in when his wife stroked his hair.

"She told me she was sorry and she loved me, but our love was selfish. She'd disgraced her family and I'd cut myself off from mine. How could we give a child a good, loving life? She had to do what was best and right for the baby, so she was going to a quiet place where her parents wouldn't be disgraced, dishonored. And she was giving the baby to a loving family so the child we made so recklessly would have a good, safe, and happy life. She asked me to forgive her, asked me to reconcile with my family as she had with hers. Not to give up my music, to be true to myself but find a way to respect and honor my parents."

He looked back at Eve. "What did I do? Nothing. She broke my heart, but more, she closed the pieces of it off. I got drunk—a lot. Missed gigs, lost work, wallowed, and raged. I pulled it back together after a while, telling myself the hell with her. I got work and I wrote, but I couldn't get it back. By the next summer, I was dead broke. Seriously broke, mostly busking for loose change. When I pawned my guitar, I knew it was over, so I stuck out my thumb and I rode it home."

"You never told your family about Johara?"

"No. I'd had the pride kicked out of me, my heart broken, but that was mine. That part of my life was mine. I fell in line, went to work for the company, learned the ropes. I guess it's in the blood, because I had a knack for it. But I stayed sad and mad—really clung to that sad and mad—under the show. Until I met Lilith."

"Sad eyes." She leaned over to kiss the top of his head. "You had such sad eyes back then."

"You knew about Johara," Eve said.

"Bolt told me everything before he asked me to marry him. She was wrong to leave the way she did, but . . ."

"Do you still have the letter she wrote?" Eve asked.

"I kept it a long time. Years. To remind me love was a lie, dreams were illusions. That's how I felt until Lilith. I showed her the letter when I told her about Johara, the baby, then I balled it up and threw it away."

"I . . . I have it. I'm sorry, Bolt, I pulled it out of the trash and kept it. I thought maybe one day, when the child grew up, they might want to know you, find you. And I know the letter hurt you, but it was loving toward the child you'd made. She was so young and trying to do what she believed was best. So I kept it."

"You kept it." He pulled her down into his lap, pressed his face to her shoulder. "I loved her, I loved the baby we'd started, but Lilith, you're the world."

"Could I have it?" Eve asked. "Make a copy of it?"

Lilith stroked Bolt's hair. "Will it help?"

"It may."

"I'll get it. I'm so sorry." She lifted Bolton's face, touched her lips to his. "We're going to get through this, but I'm so sorry."

Still holding him, Lilith looked at Eve. "It wasn't his mother. I know her. I met Bolt because I worked for her foundation. She would never have been a part of this. If she'd known, if she'd found out after it happened, she would have gone to the police."

Bolt shot his wife a baffled look. "What are you talking about?"

Eve kept her eyes on Lilith's. "You don't say the same about his father, his grandmother."

Bolton's face went from puzzled to stunned. "You can't think— They didn't know about her. I never told them."

"Bolton." Lilith cupped his face in her hands. "Think. Do you really believe your grandmother didn't keep tabs on you back then? Didn't know about Johara? Didn't know everything?"

She rose, but kept a hand on Bolt's shoulders. "Elinor Singer is a cold, calculating woman."

"Lil—"

"I will say it," she snapped. "You know how I feel, and I know you feel the same. Status and reputation are her gods, and she's ruled this family with an iron fist."

"Not you," Bolton muttered.

"No, not me. She thought she could, and so approved of me. She was mistaken, and we coat our dislike for each other in manners. It wouldn't surprise me in the least if she'd found some way to pressure or intimidate a girl barely into her twenties, emotional, fragile, to give up her child. But Johara never got the chance to do that, did she?"

Tears spilled out of eyes hot with anger. "She loved, too. You can read it, read her own heartbreak in the letter. She came to New York, that's what you think, isn't it? She came here to tell Elinor, to tell J.B. she was keeping the baby, she wanted to make a family with Bolt, she wanted their blessing. For the sake of the child. That's what you think, isn't it?"

"What I know is she came to New York, and she was shot three times on a site owned and run by Elinor and J. B. Singer, and she was walled up there, left there for thirty-seven years."

"You can't possibly think my grandmother, my father would have . . ." Bolton trailed off. The color drained out of his face again. "Who else?" He whispered it. "Who else could have?"

"She was coming back to you, Bolt." Lilith dashed tears away from her cheeks. "I'm sure of it. They couldn't have that, couldn't allow that. She didn't meet the standards. I did—a few years later when you'd fallen in line, I did. Or so they thought. A well-educated, well-brought-up young woman from a wealthy, prominent New York family. An all-American family. Marvinia met those standards in her day."

He dropped his head in his hands. "Oh Jesus, Lil."

"If she had her way, Kincade will be obliged to select a woman by those standards—because it's the sons that matter to her." Lilith's face went feral. "She'll never get her way with mine, with ours. It eats at her to know that."

Then her eyes filled again, and she pressed a hand to her mouth. "Oh God, I hate her. I didn't realize just how much. God, Bolt. Oh God."

He got up, shakily, but wrapped his arms around her. "We'll get through it. You're right, we'll get through this. Lieutenant Dallas, do you think, do you believe, my grandmother and my father killed Johara and our child?"

"I need to follow through with this information." She had two people very much on the edge, Eve thought, and needed to be very careful not to tip them over. "We're going to pursue every avenue to find out who murdered Johara Murr, to bring them to justice. Whoever they are."

Now Eve got to her feet. "I can't stress enough how vital it is you have no communication with your family until I tell you otherwise."

"Do you think I'd warn them?"

"I think you're upset and angry and confused, and may feel the need to confront them. You need to stay back and let me do my job."

"We will. Johara deserves that, Bolt. From both of us. I'll go get the letter."

"Lil," Bolt said as she started from the room. "We were so young, and each of us so sure we were right. Not much compromise between us. I can look back and see we probably wouldn't have made it. We'd have tried for each other, and the child, we'd have tried. But love isn't enough without understanding, real respect, and a hell of a lot of compromise. We wouldn't have made it. You and me? We always will."

"Damn right we will."

He sat again. "I don't know what to think, what to feel. If my grandmother did this, if my father . . . He can't stand up to her. Few can. I tried, all those years ago. I failed. And I never really tried again until Lilith, until the kids."

He turned to Roarke with the faintest of smiles. "A strong woman will make a man of you."

"Truth. We're fortunate in ours. I'm very sorry, Bolton, for your loss. I'm glad to see you've made a family who'll let you grieve that loss."

"I only knew her surname. She didn't like talking about her family, it made her feel guilty. We had some friction about that, too. I know she had a brother—in medical school. In London, I think, but I'm not sure. Her family needs to know. I could hire investigators to find them."

"Let me use my resources for that," Eve said.

"If you find them, any of them, I'd like the chance to speak with them, if they'd agree. And if you can't find them, or something happened to them over the years, Lilith and I would like to—to make the arrangements."

"I'll let you know."

"Can you tell me? You must know. We, ah, Johara and I, weren't going to find out before the birth, but you must know."

Eve started to say the fetus was male, but saw his eyes. "A boy."

"A boy." His lips trembled, then firmed. "Thank you."

After Eve took the letter Lilith had folded in an envelope, they left the Singers and stepped out into the quickening rain.

"You trust them not to make that contact."

"Yeah, I do. Especially since we're going to move fast now. Get us a copter." She looked up at the boiling sky as she got into the car. "There's more than one storm coming."

22

WHILE ROARKE DROVE, EVE TAGGED PEABODY AND SNAPPED OUT ORDERS. "Don't ask questions, just listen. Contact the local LEOs in Hudson Valley and inform them I'm on my way there, to arrest Elinor and J. B. Singer on suspicion of murder."

"Holy—"

"Shut up. The warrant will include bringing Marvinia Singer in for questioning. There will be a search warrant. As the murder took place in New York City, I will transport the individuals and any evidence found to New York City. They are to do nothing, I mean nothing, until I arrive. They are not to approach, not to enter, not to do anything. Whoever's in charge can contact me for details if deemed necessary."

"Got it. Should I meet you at the heliport?"

"No time. Get to Central, set things up there. I'll write up what I can on the flight there—God help us all. Shit, contact Mira. I want her in Observation. I may need a shrink on this. Contact Baxter, tell him and Trueheart they're on the search. They can drive. Give them the particulars. And have them pick up McNab for the electronics."

"Got it."

"Good. Go." She clicked off, tagged Reo. "Warrants, now. Listen."

She banged out details, continued to bang them out as she ran through the rain to the waiting copter.

She heard the helipad guy say, "It's going to be rough up there, sir."

"Too rough for clearance?" Roarke asked.

"No, but rough enough."

"I'll see you at Central, Reo. I have to keep a jet-copter from crashing with the strength of my will."

"You're taking a chance—with the arrests, and the flight. Let's have good luck on both."

"Yeah, let's." She strapped in. "This is a bigger machine than Peabody and I took this afternoon."

"I assumed you'd be transporting prisoners on the return."

"That's right." She tried not to think about what he did with switches and monitors or who he talked to on the headset. "It's not raining that hard."

"Not here."

She closed her eyes as the jets wound up. "Oh shit."

"I've got you, Lieutenant. Reo meant you're taking a chance, as you don't have hard evidence so much as circumstantial."

"Piles of circumstantial now. And I'm betting on a seventy-five, maybe eighty percent chance the gun that killed Johara Murr's in that big, ugly house."

"Is it ugly? And why do you think they kept the gun?"

He was keeping her talking as they rose into the air. Good idea, she decided.

"Strict and stern, Peabody said. She's right. You'll see for yourself."

Everything shook, including the contents of her stomach. "And the gun's power. I didn't find a collector's license or any record of a license in the past for that weapon. It probably came down through the family."

"Licenses, bugger licenses. We're too important for that."

"Yeah, that's it." She saw lightning flash in a giant five-pronged fork in the distance. The shake and roll of the answering thunder made her seriously consider curling into a whimpering ball.

"You see Elinor pulling the trigger."

Talk, talk, keep talking. Why wasn't she on the ground somewhere, battling a rampaging horde of chemi-heads hopped up on Zeus?

"J.B. could have done it if his ass was on the line—the way I had it playing out. Knocked her up, get rid of her. But for this? He wouldn't have the guts. Oh, fuck, fucking fuck, there's another one."

"We're fine."

She risked a glance at him. He looked calm—calm, determined, and focused. Which meant more than the strength of her will kept them aloft.

"I know what I saw in Elinor Singer today." It wasn't easy to keep her voice as calm as his, but she worked on it. "But I got a look through Lilith's lens. She's a tyrant. On top of the rest. What Lilith didn't add on the standards? White and Christian. Johara fell short on those, too. Maybe you don't have to be really religious, or totally pure, but a young, Lebanese, Muslim pianist? That would never do. She's not going to be able to pull Bolton back, get him firm under the thumb if he makes a life with that substandard girl and their illegitimate child."

She pulled in a breath, let it out slowly. "I have to ask. How much longer before we land?"

"About five minutes." He reached over, gave her hand a squeeze. "We're coming into the rough part now."

"Coming into? Fuck me sideways."

"Let's try that one once we're home again."

They bounced, swayed, jittered. She heard Roarke swear—lightly, and under his breath, but she heard it. They dipped, they danced, and a line of ice-cold sweat slid down Eve's spine.

The world outside the windscreen rolled thick and dense and dirty gray. All angry clouds snarling, booming.

Peabody would pick it up, she told herself. If they ended up a smoking, smoldering tangle of body parts and twisted copter in the river, Peabody would see it through. Justice would be done.

That was something.

Then a few tiny tears ripped through the solid gray, and through them she saw the flicker of lights from the heliport.

Roarke communicated with somebody, got clearance, and, after a couple of final, nasty shakes, they landed.

"There now."

Eve held up a finger, then dropped her head between her knees. "Not gonna boot. Just need a second. Need my warrants, too. Need my goddamn warrants."

"And there, she's rounding back already. You're a bit pale yet," he told her when she straightened. "But you'll do."

She got out, resisted kissing the wet ground, and slid into the waiting all-terrain.

"Big enough for transporting." She nodded. "I'll guide you in."

"I had them program the address. Have some water. Settle yourself the rest of the way."

"Yeah, maybe. Come on, Reo. I expect some mild resistance," she continued. "The grandmother's over the century mark, and he's a coward under it, but some. Probably threats and insults, which will hurt my delicate feelings."

"You'll muddle through."

"I tend to agree with Lilith's take on Marvinia, but we don't take chances. I'd peg her as in the best shape, physically, of the three of them. We'll be sexist here. If it comes to it, I'll deal with the women, you deal with him."

"As necessary."

"You're carrying, aren't you? You're always carrying. Don't pull a weapon, for Christ's sake, but they've got security, a gate. I don't want them to know we're coming until we're there. With the warrants. Cams on the walls, about every five feet. And alarms, scanners on the gate."

"No worries."

"Got none there. Yes! And Reo scores."

"I don't like to go on auto in this weather, so . . ." He pulled over, took out his 'link. "Just under a quarter mile."

"What are you doing?"

"Scanning their system. Ah well, it's not absolute shite, but they can afford better. I'm just going to deactivate cams and alarms. If they notice, they'll likely blame the storm. There we are."

Though pleased, the cop in her frowned. "You can do that with your 'link?"

He shot her an easy smile. "It has a few handy accessories built in."

He continued to drive and when he reached the gates, hit vertical and sailed over them.

"It is very ugly. I've seen prisons—from the outside of course—with more charm."

Lights glared against the window glass, but didn't add welcome or cheer. Eve walked through the rain to the door. "Are the door cams down?"

"They are, yes."

She rang the bell. Moments later a flustered Marvinia opened it. "Oh! Hello. I thought you were the driver. The storm's taken out the security."

"Going somewhere?" Eve asked.

"Me? In this?" On an eye roll, she shook her head. "No. But J.B. is determined to head off to Capri for some sunshine. Elinor's up there trying to talk some sense into him. I've left them to it. So sorry, come in out of this horrible rain."

She stepped back. "Roarke, it's lovely to see you. I didn't expect to see anyone on a night like this. Let me take your coats."

"We're good. I need to see your husband and mother-in-law."

"Yes, of course. Come, sit down. I'll go get them. I assume you have some resolution on your investigation, and coming out on a night like this shows you're even more dedicated than I believed."

"If you could use the house 'link to ask them to come down," Eve began, when she heard J.B.'s voice.

"I don't want to wait until morning, Mother! I need to get away from all this stress."

He appeared at the top of the staircase, and froze when he saw Eve.

"I wouldn't." She saw flight in his eyes. "Nowhere to go. Come down, Mr. Singer, or I'll come up and get you. And tell your mother to get down here."

"What is this?" Marvinia put her hand on Eve's arm. "What's wrong?"

"Okay, I'll come to you." Eve started up the staircase. "James Bolton Singer, as you already know, this is the police. I have a warrant for your arrest for the murder of Johara Murr and the viable, healthy fetus she carried."

"What? What? That's crazy. Who is she talking about?"

"Marvinia." Roarke spoke softly. "Stay here."

As Eve reached the top of the stairs, turned Singer around to restrain him, Elinor strode down the corridor to the right.

"Take your hands off my son. Get out of my house."

She lifted the gun in her hand and fired.

The bullet pinged off Eve's topper. The impact—a solid punch with a sledgehammer—jerked her back, spun her to the left. As she reached for her own weapon, Roarke flew up the stairs.

The second bullet struck closer to her hip.

The pain stole her breath, had the edges of her vision blurring. Eve set her teeth, held her weapon steady.

"Fire again, you crazy bitch, and I'll drop you. I've got it on low, but at your age, it'll put you in ICU, I swear to fucking God."

"You broke into my house. I will defend myself."

"I'm a police officer. I have a warrant. Drop that weapon, or I drop you. Last chance."

Eve held out her free hand to stop Roarke from shoving in front of her, and for five humming seconds they faced off.

Elinor let the gun fall to the thick rug. "I should have aimed for your head."

"Yeah, your mistake."

She walked over, put a boot on the weapon as she cuffed Elinor's hands behind her back.

She muttered a curse as, restraints aside, Singer ran.

"I've got him," Roarke told her and had him in hand, face against the wall, in under four feet.

"Elinor Bolton Singer, you're under arrest for the murder of Johara Murr and the viable, healthy fetus she carried. You are further charged with the attempted murder of a police officer. Additional charges will include possession and use of an unlicensed firearm."

Marvinia sat on the floor at the base of the stairs, arms wrapped tight around herself, eyes moons of shock as she rocked back and forth.

"What have they done? What have they done?"

"Shut up, you foolish twit. Contact my lawyer immediately."

"Go to hell, you evil witch. Who was she? One of J.B.'s dalliances? Did he get some poor girl pregnant?"

"Johara and your son were in love, met in college," Eve said as she walked Elinor down the stairs. "They lived together, hoped to get married."

"He— But he never told me."

"It was your grandchild they killed."

"Oh, please don't say that. Please no. Oh, J.B., no. No."

"It's insane, of course this is all insane," J.B. babbled as Roarke walked him down. "A terrible mistake. Call the lawyer now, Marvinia."

She got slowly to her feet. "Oh my God, you're lying. You're lying."

"I need you to come with us, Ms. Singer."

"Don't call me that," she snapped at Eve. "Use Kincade. Am I under arrest?"

"No, ma'am, but I need you to come with us."

"Marvinia, darling—"

"I will never speak to you again." She turned away from him to Elinor. "If there is one positive note to this horror, I never have to speak to you again."

"Let's move them out. I'll start with Mother. Elinor Singer, you have the right to remain silent."

Eve read them their rights, one at a time, as they loaded them into the all-terrain.

"I need to take the weapon into evidence. I need something to put it in."

"Field kit in the cargo area," Roarke told her.

"You never miss."

As Eve pulled out the kit, Elinor spoke coldly. "You will pay for this."

"Sister, I get paid for this. But for this one, I'd do it for free."

As she walked back in, she pulled out her communicator. "Suspects in custody. Female suspect fired an illegal weapon during the arrest— two shots at the arresting officer. I'm bringing the weapon, a handgun, which I believe is a thirty-two caliber, into evidence."

"Whoa!" Peabody shouted out. "You got shot?"

"Magic topper. I'm five-by-five. On our way to the heliport."

"Safe travels. It's cleared up here."

"Thank Christ."

She went out to where Roarke waited.

"You're going to have a couple of bruises blooming like flowers under that topper."

"Yeah, I feel them."

He gripped her chin, gave it a little shake. "Mild resistance, my ass."

"Yeah, bad call on that."

"I'm surprised you didn't stun her."

"At her age, even on low, she could stroke out. I want her alive for the ten, maybe fifteen or so years she's got left."

Those bruises sang an ugly song by the time she turned the Singers over for booking and escorted Marvinia up to an interview room.

"If you'd give me a couple minutes? I'm going to leave the door open, and Roarke will stay with you. You're not under arrest. Can I get you something to drink?"

"Water, please. Just water."

"I'll bring it back."

She stepped out as Peabody walked down with an ice pack. "Even with the coat, it had to hurt."

"She caught me twice. Bitch."

"I'll get another."

"No, I'd pretty much have to sit on the other. Are you caught up enough?" She slid the pack under her topper, pressed it to her chest.

"Yeah. Reo's talking to the PA. She's using your office."

"I figure we'll take the Singers—him first—in the morning. They're lawyering, as expected, and given the time, her age, blah blah, they're going to want to wait."

"Copy that."

"But I want to talk to Marvinia, get anything we can. Then release her. She's not in this."

"Yeah, I got that, too."

"Here." She started to take off the topper, winced. "Fuck, shit, bitch! Okay. Take this back, will you, and ask Reo to join us. Damn, and bring in some water."

"No, don't toss the pack. Keep it on. It's not like she's a suspect you have to intimidate. She saw what happened, right?"

"Yeah, yeah, you're right. Okay."

She kept the pack, walked back to the interview room. "My partner's bringing you water. She and the APA will join us. Roarke, if you'd like to wait in my office."

"Can he stay? He's someone I know, at least a little. Is it all right? Would you stay?"

"Sure, he can stay." She buzzed Peabody. "We need another chair."

"She—she shot you. With a gun. I saw . . ."

"I'm wearing protective gear."

"I've never seen anyone shot. It was horrible. They, they shot that poor girl. You said she was . . . was Bolt's girl."

"I think he should tell you the details there."

"Does he know what happened now?"

"Yes."

Tears began to slide. "He may never want to see me again. How could I blame him?"

"That's not at all true." Roarke spoke up, soothing, kind. "Your daughter-in-law, nearly the first thing she said when they learned what happened is you'd never be a part of it."

"I wouldn't. I swear to you, I didn't know. She was pregnant. My grandchild." She took a breath. "She didn't meet Elinor Singer's standards, did she?"

"I don't believe so. Ms. . . . . Kincade," Eve remembered. "You met Detective Peabody. This is Cher Reo with the prosecutor's office."

"I'm sorry for your loss," Peabody said, and Marvinia burst into tears.

"I'm sorry, I'm sorry. This isn't helping. Tell me how I can help. I need to help."

"If you could think back, probably late August, early September of 2024."

"That's when it happened? Yes, I remember that time very well because J.B. and I had separated, had been separated several months. I was seriously considering divorce. We'd been fighting all the time, over Bolt, mostly, and what he was doing with his life. I wanted him to be happy, to do what he loved. They—or Elinor—wanted him back in New York, in the company. His duty, his legacy, all of that. We argued about Bolt, we argued about his mother. Even when we traveled, he spoke to her every single day. And when we came back, it was to that house."

She cracked the seal on the water, drank.

"I hate that house. Hated it from the first moment I saw it. We fought about how J.B. lived his life. He wasn't responsible back then. Or ever," she added after a moment. "Charming, sweet, romantic, but never responsible. Even when he took over Singer, Elinor ran it, or covered his irresponsibility, his mistakes."

With a murmured thanks, she took tissues Peabody offered, then mopped at her face.

"It's not love with her. It's the Bolton-Singer name, it's how it's perceived. And it's bloodline.

"I was going to ask for a divorce, try to mend fences with Bolt, and J.B. came to me, he asked me for another chance. He seemed so contrite, so eager to try to make our marriage work again. We'd take a long trip—no partying, just the two of us. We'd reconnect. I loved him, so after some time, I gave in."

She closed her eyes. "And now I see he came to me after they'd done this. He wanted me back, that cushion, wanted to get away from what he'd done. Just bury it. I let him."

"You didn't know," Eve said.

"No, but I wanted everything he said to me then to be true, so I made it true. He even promised we'd leave Bolt alone, let him try to make a go of it with his music. At least another year."

"Can J.B. lay brick?" Reo asked.

Marvinia pressed a hand to her mouth and nodded. "Certainly not very well, but his father would have insisted he learn the basics. But they spoiled him, you see. Her especially, and his father died so young really, so it was all her. That doesn't excuse him, and I won't excuse him, but she dominates him. In the last ten years or so, I've let her dominate me far too much and too often. She's a hundred and five years old. I could justify living in that house for duty. My husband's mother, my son's grandmother."

Eve took out Johara's photo. "Did you ever see her?"

"Oh, oh, is this her? Oh, she's lovely. Lovely. Bolt never told me about her."

"He will now. He told Lilith everything before they got married."

"Good, that's good." Gently, very gently, Marvinia brushed her fingertips over the face in the photo. "They have a strong marriage, they have a strong family. Wonderful children. I would have had another grandchild.

"I'll never forgive them. No punishment the law allows is enough for what they destroyed. Did she have family?"

"We're going to look into that."

She nodded. "He's weak." She cleared her throat, drank more water. "You know how to do your job, obviously, but I want to tell you because it might help you. He's a weak and selfish man. It's not love with him, either, for his mother. It's dependence, and some fear. He'll tell you everything if he's afraid, or if he thinks you'll give him something he needs. He lies. I can tell, almost always, when he lies."

"He taps his right foot," Eve commented.

"Does he?" She laughed a little. "I've never noticed. It's his eyes. I can see the lie. We've known each other almost sixty years. I can almost always see a lie in his eyes. Will I have to testify?"

"It's possible," Reo told her.

"I don't want to speak to them. Ever. I'll testify if it helps. But I won't speak to them. And God, I don't want to go back to that house."

"You should go to your son's. Stay there for now. They'll want you," Eve added when she saw the hesitation. "I'm going to have Peabody contact them, tell them you're coming. We'll have you taken there."

"They need you now, Marvinia," Roarke told her. "As much as you need them."

"Do you really believe that?"

"I know it." Roarke took her hand. "I saw it."

"Peabody, go ahead and fix this up. Reo, any more questions?"

"Not right now. We'll contact you when we need to talk again. I know this is hard for you," Reo added. "Thank you for your cooperation."

"I'll wait here with you," Roarke said.

When they stepped out, Reo looked at her 'link. "Give me a minute," she told Eve. "Elinor Singer's lawyer's demanding to speak with me."

"You want my office?"

"No, I'll take it in the lounge. It's Michael C. Breathed."

"Breathed? Why would she have a criminal attorney on tap?"

"I'll find out."

They peeled off, Reo to the lounge, Eve to her office.

Eve hit the coffee and sat to start the paperwork.

When Roarke came in, he went straight to her AutoChef, programmed more coffee. "It's difficult to watch a woman's world fall apart."

"She'll get through it." She shook her head at him when she saw the gleam of annoyance in his eyes. "I'm not being cynical, especially. I know death when I see it. It may be the first time I've watched love die, just stop breathing, but I saw it. I saw just that on her face when she understood what he'd done. She stopped loving him and she has her son, her son's family.

"She'll get through it."

"You're right about that, but it won't be easy for her."

"No, nothing's going to be easy for any of them for a while. If the Singers push this to trial, it's going to be a lot harder."

"You think they will?"

"She hired Breathed, and he's damn good at this. Not good enough," she added. "Nobody is. She shot me, twice. That gun and the bullets—from me, from Johara—are in the lab right now. They're going to match. And in the morning, I'll break J.B. So Breathed's going to want a deal. We'll see how she feels about that."

She looked over as she heard rapid heel clicks. "Here's Reo now."

Reo pointed at the coffee. "I want that." She waved Roarke away before he could go back to the AC. "I'll get it. Elinor Singer's on some committee with Breathed's wife, and Breathed and J. B. Singer golf together."

"Explains the quick turnaround," Eve said.

"In any case, Breathed's trying the we're-all-in-a-huff routine. Centenarian client dragged from her home in a storm, in the middle of the night."

"The storm was done, and it wasn't twenty-two hundred."

"I said 'trying.'" Reo gulped coffee. "She should be immediately released on her own recognizance, would even suffer the humiliation of wearing a tracker."

"No and no."

"And when he got no and no, he insisted we go tonight."

"They want to do this tonight?"

One more unexpected turn, Eve thought.

"Mira's on her way in. I was going to dump all this on her, apologize, and send her back home."

"Are you up to go tonight?"

"Abso-fucking-lutely. But she waits while I have a round with her son first."

Reo toasted with her coffee. "We're drinking out of the same pot. He's got Indina Cross—junior partner in Breathed's firm. She's good."

"Junior partner. Mother took the top cream for herself. Let's get it lined up. This is going to go long," she told Roarke.

"And should be quite a show. One I wouldn't miss. There should be popcorn in Observation."

Now Reo tapped her mug to his. "I can't tell you how many times I've said that."

23

THEY TOOK A CONFERENCE ROOM, AND ROARKE SAT BACK AND WATCHED THE four women discuss evidence, strategy, psychology.

Singer didn't have the slightest clue what he was in for.

They would, Roarke had no doubt, simply dismantle him.

Eve pushed back, came to attention when Commander Whitney strode into the room.

"Sir."

"Sit, sit." Rather than his usual suit, he wore a casual shirt in thin blue-and-white stripes and, a little to Eve's shock, jeans and high-top kicks.

And still looked every bit in command.

"Doctor, Lieutenant, Detective, Assistant Prosecutor, Roarke." He moved straight to the AutoChef. "I don't suppose this is your coffee in here, Dallas."

"No, sir. We can get that for you."

"This'll do. I'm here to observe. I haven't asked for face-to-face reports on these cases, as you not only had them well in hand, but they moved rapidly. Yet this?"

He took a hit of coffee. "When I'm informed we've made arrests within days of an investigation of remains more than three decades old, and those arrests are individuals of some status and repute, I like to study more details. Which, considering the time, I would have done from home."

He sat, drank more coffee. His wide, dark face went to stone. "However, when those details include one of those individuals firing a handgun on one of my officers, striking her twice, I'm damn well coming in. Have you had medical attention, Lieutenant?"

"I was wearing protective gear, Commander."

"A considerable number of years ago, I was wearing protective gear when I took two hits." He tapped a fist just below his breastbone. "Knocked me flat. Dr. Mira?"

"After considerable nagging, browbeating, and guilt-tripping, I convinced the lieutenant to allow me to examine the areas involved. She has severe bruising, but the portable scanner detected no fractures or internal injuries."

"All right then. Is my information correct that you intend to start the interview process on both suspects tonight?"

"At their insistence, sir," Eve told him.

He smiled. "This should be interesting. Are you observing, Roarke?"

"I am, yes, and it'll be very nice to have your company, Jack, as well as Charlotte's."

"I promised to keep Anna informed. She despises Elinor Singer. An incident twenty, maybe twenty-five years ago involving table decor at a gala." He studied his coffee. "My wife holds a grudge."

Then he smiled broadly at Roarke. "But as she's not here, we'll get snacks. And enjoy them," he added, scanning the women. "Because I have every confidence in my officers, our prosecutor, and the doctor to wrap these two up and serve them a very large, very unpleasant platter of justice."

He rose, turned to Roarke. "I want chips. There should be some salt and vinegar chips in Vending, which are now banned by Anna's decree from our home and my office. I'm buying. We'll get you a share, Dr. Mira."

"We should have fizzies with that." Roarke shot Eve a wink as he left with Whitney. "Do it up right."

A little bemused, Eve watched them walk out. "Well, that was unusual."

"He's angry," Mira said to Eve. "He's furiously angry. You were shot. He wants payment for that. He's angry, but he also trusts we'll get that payment. But trust aside, he needs to see it done."

"Peabody, have them bring J. Bolton Singer into Interview A. And let's get it done for the commander."

Singer didn't look so stylish in his orange jumpsuit. Beside him, his lawyer appeared very buttoned down, very ready to go. Indina Cross, a mixed-race female of forty-eight, wore a navy suit, a crisp white shirt, and tiny gold balls in her ears as her only jewelry.

Currently, her wide, thin mouth pressed into disapproving lines as Eve ordered the record on, read off the names, case numbers, and charges.

She pushed off first. "My client wishes to get this ridiculous interview over and done so he can return to his own home. The charges are without merit. There is no evidence supporting them or involving my client with the death of the woman purportedly identified as Johara Murr."

"First, she has not been purportedly identified, the victim's identity is confirmed, and her relationship with your client's son has been confirmed. The paternity of the fetus has been confirmed by the father—your client's son. So don't sit there and insult the victim, counselor."

"We will have our own forensic scientists examine the—"

"Fine, you do that. When we go to court. Meanwhile, she is Johara Murr and your client is the grandfather of the fetus who died with her. You're going to want to move off that one, Ms. Cross." Eve's warning filled the room with frost. "You're going to want to move off that one real quick or your client's going to be escorted back to his cell for the night, and this interview ends."

"Indina."

"The identity of the victim doesn't change the lack of evidence as applies to my client." As she spoke, she reached over to pat Singer's hand.

Indulgently, Eve noted.

"She was murdered, shot three times, in early September of 2024 on a property owned by your client and his company. She was concealed by a hastily built brick wall in a building under construction on property owned by your client. She was in a serious, committed relationship with your client's son, and carrying a child from that relationship.

"These are facts."

"As it's impossible to establish the exact date this unfortunate incident occurred—"

"Between September seventh and September twelfth, according to the records of the building under construction. It's the wall, J.B., it's all about the wall. The bricks. When they were ordered, delivered, used."

"And you have job reports, invoices, and so on from this time?"

"Your mother's a sharp businesswoman, isn't she? I bet she kept records. And I bet the search team, the very skilled e-man on it, will find those records in her files. They're searching right now."

"They can't go into our home!" Singer snatched at Cross's arm. "They can't just go into our home, go through our things. It's insulting."

"Warrant." Reo opened her file, slid it across the table.

"I didn't order any bricks. You won't find anything about them."

"But you laid them. You built that wall."

He smiled, held out his soft, pampered hands. "My dear girl, do I look like a bricklayer?"

Eve smiled back. "I'm not your dear girl. And no, you don't. That's why you did a sloppy job. Did it bother you at all as you laid those courses? Did it make you just a little sick seeing her lying there, knowing what was dying inside her? Part of you, dying inside her, did that trouble you at all?"

"My client categorically denies knowing the victim, knowing of the victim, of having any knowledge of her death. All you have is innuendo and circumstantial."

"I've got the thirty-two-caliber handgun, the two bullets that hit me tonight from said weapon, and the three recovered from the remains of Johara Murr."

"And the ballistic reports?"

"Waiting on that."

Cross let out a soft sound of dismissal, but Eve looked at Singer. "You know they're going to match."

"I know no such thing."

She nodded as she heard the quiet tap of his foot on the floor. "You know they're going to match, just as you knew, and feared, we were going to find out who the woman you and your mother murdered was, her connection to your son. The son who wept for her tonight."

"I don't know anything about it." Tap, tap, tap. "I imagine Bolton had relationships, as any young man might, with any number of women he met in college."

"I didn't say they met in college."

"I assumed."

"You don't care about him, either," Peabody put in. "Your own son, his pain or grief. That's just sad."

"You know nothing about it."

"You haven't asked about him at all, or about your wife." Peabody jabbed a finger at him. "You haven't shown any concern for Johara or the baby. Nothing. Because you don't feel anything for any of them. That's why it was easy for you to kill her."

"I didn't kill anyone!"

"You were running," Eve reminded him. "When we arrived at your home tonight, you were packing to fly out, to run."

"My client planned to take a trip, a break from the stress of the last several days. It's not a crime."

Eve ignored the lawyer. "You tried to run. Your mother tried to kill me, and you tried to run."

"You burst into our home. You frightened her. Obviously, she believed you were an intruder and put hands on me. She tried to defend me, and herself."

"Left your wife off that one, too. Your wife, who opened the door for me. My partner and I had been in your home only hours before. You and your mother knew who I was, a police officer. I announced same, informed you and your mother you were being arrested and why. And yet she fired on me."

"We were confused, obviously. It happened very quickly. In any event, I didn't have a weapon. I didn't fire a weapon."

Time to toss Mother aside, Eve decided.

"You knew about Johara, about the baby, because your mother holds on tight. Johara came to you, didn't she, desperate to have you accept her, the child, so she could have a hope of making a family with your son. She needed your blessing, your support. Maybe she couldn't get that from her family—we'll find out. But as she came closer to term, she wanted family for the child. She wanted a father for the child, so came to you for your blessing."

"Nonsense."

This time he couldn't meet her eyes as he lied.

"So you and your mother had her come to the site—a handy place to kill and conceal the body. No one would know. Everyone would forget her. Bolton wanted music, and he refused to take his place in the business. So you told her to come there. Look at what we do, what we build, what we want for Bolt. That would be a pretty good way to lure her there.

"Then you shot her, watched her fall."

"I did not. I did not."

"And built the wall, poured the ceiling. Gone, forgotten, finished. But here's the thing about the walls, J.B. You're no bricklayer, you're right about that. Sloppy work. I'm betting you were pretty shaken while you built it on top of being crap at it. How many times, I wonder, did you scrape your knuckles? Work gloves? But even with those, you banged your hands, maybe an elbow. You bled a little here and there."

He thought about that, Eve noted. Sweat started to pool as he tried to think, to remember. "We're testing every brick, and we're going to find your DNA. And when we do, what happens, APA Reo?"

"What happens is Mr. Singer does two consecutive life sentences in a small, unpleasant cage in an off-planet facility. The fetus was healthy at the TOD, the fetus was viable outside the womb at TOD. Two life sentences and your attorney knows when we find that DNA, and we will, that's a slam dunk."

"His attorney is very confident her client's DNA will not be found, as Mr. Singer had no part in constructing the aforesaid wall."

"Did Mommy help you?" Peabody wondered. "Or did you do it all by yourself?"

Singer leaned over, whispered in Cross's ear.

"Of course. I need a few moments with my client."

"No problem. Dallas, Peabody, and Reo exiting Interview to accommodate counsel. Record off. Anybody want a snack?" Eve said, deliberately carefree as they left. "Peabody, use my code and get us some chips."

"Really?" Peabody said when the door closed.

"Actually, yeah. And something to wash them down. This isn't going to take as long as I thought."

Mira came out of Observation, hurried toward them. "He's lying, of course, but even in the relatively short time of the interview his skill for lying is eroding."

"The DNA on the bricks did it," Reo concluded. "Good call there, Dallas."

"It might even be true. He's worried it's true. He's afraid of prison."

"He should be. And he's sure as hell going there."

"But you'll make the deal."

Reo spared Eve a glance before she put her hands together for Peabody and her armload of chips and sodas. "Yes! I want!"

"I started to get veggie chips for me, then I thought, screw that. I've earned these calories today."

"You'll make the deal," Eve repeated as she opened her bag of chips.

"Twenty to twenty-five, minimum, on-planet. We discussed this, Dallas."

"I'm not giving you grief over it. We both know it's the mother pulling the strings. He rolls, he lays it all out, he can have the deal. He'll probably die in prison anyway." She crunched into a chip. "I'm not sorry about that. I don't know if he pulled the trigger—I lean, especially after tonight, toward her on that. But he's just as responsible."

"You should take a blocker," Mira told her.

"No. Feeling the hits keeps me mean. How's it going in Observation?"

"Jack—the commander—is enjoying himself—and the chips. He liked your sad outrage, Peabody."

Peabody lit right up. "Really?"

"I wonder what this grudge is Anna Whitney has on Elinor Singer?" Eve turned as the interview door opened.

And saw, immediately, Cross's mouth had gone thin again.

"My client has certain information he's willing to share, on record, for a dismissal of charges against him."

"That's a no. Cross, don't waste my time."

Cross stared hard at Reo. "I believe my client has information valuable to your investigation. In consideration of same—"

"You want to talk deal, we can talk deal. Depending on the information, the value thereof, and your client's full disclosure of his part and participation in the murder of Johara Murr and the viable fetus. We both know he's guilty. Again, it's late. Don't waste our time."

Eve handed what was left of her bag of chips to Mira. "Add this to the pile. If you're ready to get going again, counselor, we'll get going. Otherwise, your client goes back to his cell, and we bring up his mother. She may be more forthcoming."

She added a shrug. "First come, first dealt."

"We resume the interview."

Eve took the tube of Pepsi with her. "Record on. Resuming Interview with Singer, J. Bolton, and counsel. Dallas, Peabody, Reo entering Interview. Okay, J.B., spill it."

"Immunity—"

"Is off the table." Reo let out a sigh. "If your counsel is worth her fee, she explained to you we wouldn't make that deal."

"Five to ten," Cross said briskly, "in a low-security facility on-planet."

This time Reo just laughed. "You want us to give him a ride in a country club rehabilitation center? He murdered a woman and her thirty-two-week-old fetus."

"I didn't kill anyone! She did!"

"J.B." Cross gripped his arm. "You need to be quiet. My client has information regarding the death of Johara Murr. He is over eighty years old. Even a ten-year sentence is prohibitive and extreme. I believe any court would agree—"

"Then let's take it to court." Eyes glittering, Reo leaned forward. "You want to risk that, you'd risk that, knowing what he told you? What his wife told us?"

"You spoke with Marvinia! She can't say anything about it. We're married."

"Shut up, J.B. Fifteen years, on-planet, low security."

"Listen up. Twenty to twenty-five, on-planet, max security. And this is contingent on whether the information your client has is viable, valuable, and truthful. There will be no negotiation on those terms. If I take this to court, he will serve two life sentences, off-planet. Take the deal or don't, because he's just the type of defendant I like to prosecute."

"Indina. Twenty years!"

After a study of Reo's face, Cross turned to Singer. "I'm advising you to take this deal. On-planet, J.B. You'll have a chance to serve this time and get out, and live."

"But my God, my God." He held out his hands to Eve. "You have to understand, have some pity. I was coerced, I was in shock. I was afraid."

"Are you, on advice of counsel, taking the deal currently on the table?" Eve asked him.

"Yes, yes, I'll take it, if you promise you'll consider what I tell you, and my state of mind. If you promise to consider all of that and have some pity, perhaps renegotiate."

"We'll consider everything. Tell us about the murder of Johara Murr."

"It all goes back, you see. We were all worried about Bolt. He had this delusion he could make a living with his music. His mother went against us on this and indulged him. An obvious mistake, as he had a legacy, a duty here, and to the company his great-grandfather had started."

Duty, Eve thought. Legacy. Elinor Singer's words, no question.

"You kept tabs on him."

"My mother, thinking of his best interest, hired an agency to watch out for him."

"So she knew, you knew, when he became involved with Johara Murr."

"Yes, of course. Mother was upset, as you can imagine. She wasn't even an American, but I convinced Mother to let it go. Boys will be boys, after all. Even when it seemed to be more serious, we felt we should let it run its course. He was so stubborn, you see. If we forbade him from seeing her, living with her, it would only cement the connection. But then they were careless. She got pregnant."

"That must've been a blow," Peabody commented.

"It was impossible, of course. He was far too young and foolish. She was completely inappropriate. I expected her to terminate the pregnancy, then began to see, as Mother had, that she used it to trap him. That's why Mother went to London to speak to her parents."

Of course she had, Eve thought. "Elinor went to Johara's parents?"

"They were very unhappy to hear of the relationship and the pregnancy and, on Mother's advice, put on a bit of pressure to convince the girl to come home, to visit."

"Without telling her why."

"She was, as I understand, a very obedient young woman. When she went to them, they convinced her, as they should have, the relationship had to end, that she was far too young to raise a child, that she had disgraced the family. She agreed to go to her aunt, and to put the child up for adoption. A good home, of course. A stable home."

"But she changed her mind."

"We believe the aunt eventually told her about my mother's visit to her parents, and irresponsibly supported her change of mind, and her coming to New York. She was upset we'd interfered, and tried to convince my mother—whom she rightfully saw as the head of the family—that she and Bolton loved each other and the child."

He cleared his throat. "You have to understand, I had no idea what Mother planned when she insisted the girl meet us at the site. I believed it was to show her the scope of what the family stood for, what Bolton was part of. How misguided it was to push him off this path.

"And then we were there. It was a beautiful night, I remember, a beautiful night, the girl said how passionate Bolt was about his music. How he needed a chance to reach his potential. If we loved him, as she did, we'd support him. She—she said she was going to him, going to beg him to forgive her for leaving, and she would tell him everything we'd done.

"And Mother shot her."

He paused, covered his face with his hands. "I didn't know. I didn't. I was so shocked! She fell, and Mother said, 'Push her in. Push the tramp and her bastard in.'"

"And did you?" Eve asked.

"Yes. God forgive me. Yes. I didn't know what else to do. One of her shoes, and her purse, they didn't go in like she did. Mother picked them up. She said to go down and build the brick wall. She would mix the mortar."

"So you built the wall together."

"I didn't have a choice!" J.B. stretched his hands out, looked at Eve with a face full of fear and sorrow. "It was already done. It was too late, and we had to protect the family. She shouldn't have come back, she shouldn't have threatened us. Mother even offered her a hundred thousand dollars to go back, but she refused.

"I was sick, the whole time, just sick. Mother said for me to go to Marvinia and convince her to repair our marriage, and to agree to give Bolton another year or so. He'd come back, she'd see to it. So I did, and he did, and everything was fine again."

"Everything was fine again."

"Was it?" Eve shot back again. "Was everything fine for Johara and her child? For your son?"

"He has a very good life, the right kind of life. He would never have had a good life with this girl. She used him, she threatened us."

"Is that it?" Eve demanded.

"Yes, it's the truth. None of this would have happened if Bolt hadn't decided, without consulting us, to sell that property to Roarke. No one would have remembered her. Surely you must see I was given no choice. I didn't kill that unfortunate girl."

"At the very least, you were and are an accessory."

"And the deal stands—as long as it's proven out." Reo looked at Cross. "Are we done here?"

Cross merely lifted her hands.

"Then let's go to a conference room, make it official."

"But—but—I told you everything. You can see I was coerced. I didn't know. You have to have some pity."

Eve rose. "Sorry, all my pity's used up. It's all for Johara Murr. Interview end."

Eve took twenty minutes to recharge by sitting in her office, boots on her desk.

She turned her head into Roarke's hand when he came in, laid it on her hair.

"One wonders," he said, "the genetic miracle that makes a man like Bolton Singer with such a father, such a grandmother."

"We'd know about that."

"We would. You should take a blocker."

"Not yet. This last round won't take long. She's either going to spew or clam up and go to court. Either way, we've got her."

"You hope to make her spew."

"I'm going to give it a damn good shot." She sat up, rolled her shoulders when her communicator signaled.

"Tell me the good stuff."

"I've got good stuff," McNab told her. "I want to make out like it was hard, like I had to pull out super magic skills, but it's all on her office comp. Yeah, passcoded, but not much more. It goes back decades. But I've scanned through, and I can give you a whole bunch that ties her up in this."

"Gimme. Send it. I'm about to put her in the box."

"Really? It's almost midnight."

"She wants it."

"Okay then, I'm going to give you the cherry on top. Trueheart found a passport in the name of Johara Murr in Elinor Singer's bedroom safe. Now, I did have to use some magic to open it. So credit there."

"Sick, sociopathic bitch. I need a copy of everything. Listen, if you want to break for the night after that, you're cleared for a hotel."

"I think we're into it, but we might want one after we're done."

"Good enough. Keep me informed. Good work, McNab. Good work all around."

"She kept the passport," Roarke said quietly. "So she could take it out, look at it, congratulate herself for seeing that the family line continues as she dictated."

"Yeah. Why don't you let Mira know about that? I need to— Busy around here," she said when her computer signaled an incoming. "What goes on top of the cherry on top?"

"Those sprinkles things?" he suggested. "Those colorful little candies?"

"We just got sprinkles."

Peabody stepped in. "She's up."

"So are we. Grab Reo. We need a few minutes before we take her."

Roarke read the screen over Eve's shoulder. "I'll update Mira and Jack. Take her down hard, Lieutenant."

"You bet your fine ass."

The jumpsuit didn't flatter Elinor any more than it did her son. She looked her age, at least around the eyes. Her very distinguished counsel sat in his very distinguished suit at her side as Eve started the record, read in the data.

"It's late, so why not make this quick? You're going to want to wait, Mr. Breathed," Eve added as he started to speak. "Just hold on to all the objections, the my client this and that. First, Mrs. Singer, your son just rolled all over you and back again."

"That's absurd."

"That's fact. I have his statement, and his confession and his play-by-play on record, and we'll get to that. Next, we have records accessed from your home office computer for a pallet of bricks to be delivered to the site and the building under construction where the remains of Johara Murr and her fetus were found. Your order, signed by you, for said bricks and for the mortar required to build the ten-by-eighteen-foot wall, dated September 8, 2024."

"Really, Lieutenant, Mrs. Singer, without a doubt, ordered material for that site and many others. This is hardly evidence of murder."

"She ordered the brick for a wall that was not on the blueprints, not in the plans, and was used to conceal the body of Johara Murr. Just wait, will you?" she snapped at Breathed. "Here, I have a copy of a passport found during the warranted search of your home.

Found in your bedroom safe. A passport in the name of Johara Murr. Maybe you'd like to tell us how you came to be in possession of this item?"

"I know nothing about it."

"It just, what, popped in there by magic? It has a stamp on her entry to New York. It's dated September 8, 2024. The same day you ordered the brick—rush delivery, I'll add. Cost you extra." She pushed the copy across the table.

"I'll need a moment with my client."

"Fine, fine, but can you just wait until I'm finished piling on the evidence, so we can get the hell out of here sometime tonight? I have here the ballistic report—I can rush things, too—on the weapon you used to fire two shots at me, a police officer, this evening."

"My client was confused, and believed you were an intruder attacking her son."

"That's bullshit, as the record, which I'll play, clearly shows. You thought about trying that third shot, but you knew I'd stun you. I didn't stun you because you're really old and it could've killed you, even on low. But you really wanted to fire again, try for the head shot. Even better than the—on-record—attempted murder of a police officer, which will get you twenty-five to life, is the fact that the bullets fired from that gun tonight and the bullets fired thirty-seven years ago into Johara Murr match. Same weapon used. You should've gotten rid of it. Shouldn't have kept her passport, should've destroyed those invoices, but you didn't want to. They were like medals of honor for you."

"You won't put me in prison."

"Elinor, we need to talk."

She shoved Breathed's hand away. "She will not put me in prison. Do you know who I am?"

"Oh, yes, I do. You bet I do."

"You broke into my home, you planted all those things. I will be believed over you. You're nothing. You're married to a competitor, a criminal. Everyone knows he's no more than a vicious Irish thug. You're trying to destroy what my family has built over generations for him, for some nouveau riche foreigner. People will believe me."

"Not a chance. Your own lawyer doesn't believe that line of bullshit. Science, you murdering bitch. Science, evidence, statements. A recording that shows you holding the weapon, firing it at me, just like you fired on the pregnant woman your grandson loved."

"Love means nothing. She was some tramp, some whore trying to worm her way into my family, our status, our money, our heritage with the bastard growing inside her."

"Your great-grandchild," Peabody mumbled.

"Nothing but a nit."

"Elinor, stop. My client has nothing more to say at this time."

"She thinks she can bully me." Elinor pushed his hand away again. "That whore thought the same. She found out differently, and so will you."

"So you shot her, killed her, had your son help you wall her in because you considered her a whore and the child inside her a nit that had to be killed so as not to infect your family."

"She was a threat. I eliminated the threat. That is my right as head of the family. You will not put me in prison for protecting my family from infestation."

"You'll never know another day of freedom," Eve promised.

"No, she won't," Reo agreed. "There will be no deal, Mr. Breathed, so let's not waste time on that. Your client has confessed. We have evidence on top of evidence. She will serve her two life sentences for murder and her twenty-five for attempted murder of a police officer, consecutively."

"Ms. Reo, consider my client's age and life expectancy."

"She'll live that expectancy out in prison. One concession I'll give, considering that age and the physical strain of transporting her off-planet, is she'll live what's left of her life in an on-planet maximum-security prison.

"Take me to court on it," Reo invited. "And that concession is deleted." She rose. "Speak with your client, but that's it, and that's all."

She sailed out.

"Reo exiting Interview." Eve rose, gathered the files. "We actually have more, but you get the gist. When you've finished with your client, she'll be taken back to her cell."

"I will not spend another minute in that hellhole."

"You're going to spend a lot more than a minute in hellholes. I only wish you had more years left to spend in them. Interview end."

Epilogue

EVE STEPPED OUT, RUBBED HER FINGERS ON HER GRITTY EYES, THEN OVER her face, then back into her hair.

She needed a shower, she thought, needed to wash off the sludge that excuse for a human had left behind.

"You sure called it, going for the son first." Peabody scrubbed at her own face. "Not only the way he rolled, but getting the time to get the ballistics, to have the search come around. Her lawyer barely got to play lawyer."

"He might try to push a little more, but I'm not budging." Reo bared her teeth at the closed door of Interview A. "Neither is the boss. I'll take a conference room if he wants to play with it awhile. She may overrule him. She may insist on going to trial."

"She may," Mira agreed as she walked to them. "She's a malignant narcissist, classic, and is certain she will never face consequences."

"She will, and there'll be more of them if she takes it to court. Either way." Reo rolled her shoulders. "Long day."

"He's going to push for bail, or house arrest."

Reo nodded at Eve. "He will, and he'll do so knowing he won't get either. The passport? That's gold. But the diamonds and rubies on the gold? She used the same gun she used to kill a twenty-two-year-old woman pregnant with her own great-grandchild to shoot a cop."

Nothing could have satisfied Eve more. "Now I'll take a blocker. Who has one?"

Peabody reached in her pocket, Reo in her briefcase, Mira in her purse. "Jesus, really? You all carry them?"

She plucked one from Peabody, knocked the tiny blue pill back.

"Ice those bruises," Mira told her.

"I appreciate you coming in for this. I know it all ran late."

"I wouldn't have missed it. Breathed will most certainly try to convince her to submit to a psychiatric evaluation, but she'll dismiss that. Nothing wrong with her. I'm going to rewatch those recordings, both of them, the first chance I have. Fascinating. I may do a paper on them. But for now, I'm going home. Dennis probably waited up, and, if so, we're going to have some midnight ice cream and talk this through."

"Midnight ice cream?"

"A family tradition. It's been a pleasure, in our way, to work with all of you on this. Get some rest."

"I'll wait this out," Reo said as Mira walked away. "No need for you to stay."

"I need to write it up."

"Write it up in the morning, which it already is. This was good work," Reo added. "Better than good work, but I'm getting a little punchy, and that's the best I can do."

"Don't let him string you out too long."

"Oh, believe me, Dallas, he knows she's cooked. See you next time."

"I'm just going to write up the broad strokes," Eve told Peabody as they headed back. "We can fill it in in the morning. Take an hour personal time there. Sleep in a little."

"Whole bed to myself."

"Right. We'll give you a lift home."

"I wouldn't mind it."

"Give me ten minutes."

Broad strokes, she told herself as she sat at her desk. And God, even she'd had enough coffee. She got water and laid down those broad strokes.

"Haven't you had enough for tonight?" Roarke walked in.

"Yeah, I have. I'm going to finish in the morning. I figured you were still playing with the commander, so I'd get started."

"He said to tell you very fine work, and he'd like to see you in his office tomorrow. Late morning. He was talking to Anna when he left. I believe she's very pleased."

"Well, that was the whole goal, pleasing the commander's wife."

She rose, looked at him, then moved into him.

"There now, my darling Eve."

She held on, and tight. "There are horrible people in the world. Ugly people, vicious people, but there aren't, under all that, so many genuinely evil people. Elinor Singer is one of them."

"She is, yes. She tried to take you from me. My heart stopped, just an instant. Even as I was moving, there was no breath in me."

"She tried, she failed. You gave me magic. You're not an Irish thug, but even if you were, I'd love you anyway."

Such was her fatigue she didn't hear Peabody clomping to her office until she heard her partner's: "Awww!"

"Shut up, Peabody."

But she kept holding on.